Under
The Screaming Field

Wendyter

In the Under the Bedclothes series:

Tales Told After Lights Out *Pat Thomson*
Bump in the Night *Mary Hoffman*

In the Nightmares series:

Horrorscopes *Nicholas Adams*
IOU *Nicholas Adams*
Class Trip *Bebe Faas Rice*
Nightmare Inn *T. S. Rue*
Deadly Stranger *M. C. Sumner*
The Teacher *Joseph Locke*

STORIES UNDER THE BEDCLOTHES

THE SCREAMING FIELD

Wendy Eyton

Illustrations by
George Buchanan

Lions

An Imprint of HarperCollins *Publishers*

First published in Great Britain in Lions 1993
2 4 6 8 10 9 7 5 3

Lions is an imprint of HarperCollins Children's Books,
a division of HarperCollins Publishers Ltd,
77–85 Fulham Palace Road,
Hammersmith, London W6 8JB

ISBN 0 00 674663-2

Printed and bound in Great Britain by
HarperCollins Manufacturing, Glasgow

For Harry

The setting of *A Pocket of Posies* is the village of
Eyam in Derbyshire,
but the story is *not* that of the Eyam plague.

CONTENTS

The Screaming Field

On a cloudless, warm June day – that was when they first heard it.

Mum had gone on the special shopping bus to Sheffield with Aunty Brenda and left them sandwiches, so they decided to make a picnic and take Sky, their border collie, over to Gants Field.

Gants Field was just outside the village – it bordered the moorland, where clusters of grey sheep moved amongst purpling heather. They could not take Sky onto the moors because he would charge towards the sheep, trying to round them up. Now he trotted lightly through the village, pausing every so often to flatten himself on the ground.

There were no sheep in Gants Field and the only building in sight was a derelict farmhouse. The field was surrounded by a stone wall, crumbling in places and so easy to climb over, even for Maisie. Tom, her older brother, gave her a leg up and a push. Then he handed over the box with the picnic in it. Sky was already in the field. He had his own way of getting in and out of places. He ran around with his tail hanging low, sniffing at the ancient stones.

Gants Field was full of stones. Great lumps of blackened, pock-marked limestone, weirdly shaped. One looked like a giant's disfigured face, one a prehistoric lizard, rearing up out of the earth. Maisie's favourite was a stone covered in lichen and bloated out like a huge toad. She sat down by it and started pulling off her shoes and socks.

"I'm melted," she said.

Tom pushed about in the box for the orange-juice carton. They ate their picnic, throwing lumps of sandwiches to Sky. A bird skimmed a nearby copse with a joyful, bubbling sound.

"That's a curlew," said Tom.

Maisie lay back in the cool grass. Her fingers picked at the tiny harebells. She gazed at the blue vastness overhead. Tom handed her a chocolate bar with turkish delight inside. Maisie nibbled at the chocolate round the edges, saving the best for last.

And then they heard it. The terrible screaming. There in Gants Field, in the still heat of the noonday sun, with the rising and falling song of the lark and the bees rummaging unconcernedly in clover. The hackles on Sky's back rose and he whimpered uneasily. Maisie sat up, staring in horror at Tom.

What was it? Where did it come from?

They listened tensely and, after a minute of silence, the screaming started again. Tom stood up, his face pale under his tan.

"It must be a fox," he said. "Caught in a trap."

But the screaming was everywhere, all around them, and it did not sound like a fox. It sounded *almost* human.

This happened when Maisie was eight years old, and Tom eleven. In the two years that followed, houses were built on Gants Field.

There was some protest about it in the village, particularly from people who had moved there from the south. The field, they said, was of geological interest and should be protected by law. Angry letters were written to the planning officer at the Town Hall, who, some said, had been to school with the man who wanted to build the houses. Eventually it was agreed that the derelict farmhouse should be demolished and six houses built on the upper part of the field, but that the lower part, with the stones on, should remain untouched. Grumblings continued, and letters to the local paper, but the big yellow bulldozers moved in just the same.

The houses, when finished, stuck out like so many concrete thumbs on the brow of the hillside. Local people referred to them en masse as "the bottle factory". There was a slump in the property market and, after six months, only one house had been sold. The couple who bought it were rumoured to have come from Sheffield, but no one knew for sure. They did not mix with the local people, and rarely visited The Pig of Lead.

The Pig of Lead was the local public house, run by Tom and Maisie's mother and father. Nearly all the people in the village went there at some time or other and one of their favourite customers was Mick, the local policeman.

Mick looked very different off duty, in his jogging suit and trainers. He organized football games at Tom's school. He was also very good at telling stories, and knew all the local legends.

The Screaming Field

It was Mick who told Tom and Maisie about the Screaming Field. He said they were not the only ones to have heard the terrible sound. "Over the years several people have reported strange screamings to the police," he said, "to the local paper, and even to the RSPCA. But there's never been any trace of an injured animal or human in Gants Field, or in the ruined farmhouse, or the countryside round about."

The farm, according to Mick's story, once belonged to a farmer called Joseph Gant. To protect his crops he used to set traps for rabbits in Gants Field – cruel, harsh traps with metal teeth which snapped the leg of the unsuspecting animal and kept it captive often for a whole night long, as Farmer Gant went to empty the traps only when the fancy took him. Gant had married a young woman called Rosa, a little mouse-like creature who, it was said, never dared to contradict him. But Rosa would lie awake at night listening for the sound of a poor animal in distress and she would often, with Joseph Gant snoring his head off on the pillow, put on a shawl, steal out into the night and struggle with the traps until her hands bled.

But one night there was a screaming so loud, and so insistent, that half the village heard it

11

and even Joseph Gant stopped his snoring and leapt out of bed. His wife, Rosa, was nowhere in the house, so he pulled on his coat and, swearing mightily, crunched through Gants Field in the moonlight where the bracken shone ghostly white and the great black stones seemed to wait in judgement on him.

"The screaming had stopped by then," said Mick, "but he found a large leveret in one of the traps and the poor thing was dead, with one of its legs broken. Joseph Gant carried the dead leveret home and flung it into a corner of his kitchen, bellowing again for his wife Rosa, who still was nowhere to be found."

At this point he glanced at Maisie, uncertain whether to continue.

But, "Was she dead?" demanded Maisie, not batting an eyelid.

"Well, yes," said PC Mick. "When Joseph Gant went into the kitchen the next morning there was no leveret on the floor, but his wife lying dead and with her leg broken."

"Had the leveret turned into his wife, then?" asked Maisie, wide-eyed. "Was it really his wife in the trap?"

"So the story goes," said Mick. "It was his punishment, you see. A bit unfair on Rosa, I can't help thinking. But it's only a legend. I

don't suppose things happened that way at all.
Joseph Gant died soon afterwards – some say
of a broken heart, because although a brutal
man he had loved his wife. The farm became
derelict, and no one has lived on Gants Field
since."

"Until now," said Maisie.

Tom looked at PC Mick thoughtfully. "But
who punished him?" he said.

Although Maisie had listened to the story without showing signs of being upset, she slept
badly that night. She went on the next day
about animals being caught in traps.

"They don't set those gin-traps for animals
now," said her mother, buttering toast. "It's
against the law. If you hear a fox crying out
these days, it's probably the mating season."

"There's some that do even worse things to
animals than set traps," said their father grimly,
shaking the local paper.

"Come on, you two, you'll be late for school,"
said their mother. She gave her husband a kick
under the table and Tom noticed it, although
Maisie did not. Later, looking through the
paper, he found the article about badger
baiting.

★ ★ ★

That evening, to everyone's surprise, the man from the new house on Gants Field visited The Pig of Lead. He was a big man, dark and swarthy, and had with him three men whose accents were different from the village people's. Not Birmingham, thought Tom to himself, but Sheffield perhaps, or even Manchester.

Tom was sitting in a quiet corner of the pub, doing his homework. He could see the four men clearly. Three of them were cracking jokes and making a lot of noise, but the man from Gants Field sat impassively. He had two terriers with him, and when Sky approached them the dogs yapped and snarled ferociously. The man from Gants Field gave one of the dogs a vicious kick and, winded, it crawled underneath the table.

Tom's mother, who was collecting ash trays and emptying them, called Sky over to the end of the room where Tom was sitting.

"We don't want him involved with those little brutes," she whispered. "They've been in several fights by the look of them."

Tom thought that any dog at the receiving end of a kick like that could hardly help being a brute. Something was beginning to tick away at the back of his brain. Something that he had read in the local paper only that morning.

14

"I'm going outside for a minute," he told his mother.

The van, when he found it, had been parked at the far end of the car park, under the shadow of a tall beech tree. The van's tax disc had faded. The number plate had been muddied over and blackened and he could not even feel what the number should be. The windows of the van were small and dirty. Tom rubbed at one with his sleeve and peered into the back of the van. He made out some straw and the outline of two garden spades. The spades were propped against a large box, and from inside the box came scratching noises. His heart began to beat quickly. The police-house was on the other side of the village from Gants Field, about ten minutes' run away. Tom ran.

He saw PC Mick through the lighted window, struggling with his paperwork. Tom knocked on the window, and Mick jumped up in surprise.

"So you think they've got a badger?" he said, when Tom had finished his story. "Muddied registration, a box, straw, dogs that look as if they've been in fights – it all adds up, doesn't it? Funny idea of sport some people have."

"Did they use the dogs to dig out the badger?" asked Tom.

"In the daytime," said Mick, "when the badgers were sleeping. And what they intend to do tonight worries me even more."

He began to put out messages on his radio.

"Now you come back to the pub with me, Tom. But don't get involved."

Tom's feeling of excitement and anticipation took a nose-dive when he and Mick arrived at the car park to find only deep rutted tyre marks where the van had been. Once on the road, it was impossible to trace. The men were no longer in the pub, of course. Tom's mother said they had left ten minutes before.

"I think I'll go and scout around a bit," said Mick. Tom begged to go too, but his mother would not hear of it.

Later, he looked out over the surrounding countryside from his bedroom window. There was a full moon shining, and he could see quite clearly the distant ridge of moorland, the wooded copses, even the stones in Gants Field.

Somewhere out there, he thought, men are baiting a captive badger. In a shed, in a pit, letting dogs loose on it.

He felt the same wave of red hot anger as

when the local hunt had chased a terrified fox across the field behind the pub. The braying hounds had later torn the fox to pieces.

Sport in the morning, sport in the evening.

Cretins, all of them.

Mick had asked Tom to keep quiet about the night's proceedings, but at school the next day he spoke to his friend, Stuart, about the people at the house on Gants Field. Stuart, he knew, did a paper round there.

"I've seen a white van parked there sometimes," said Stuart. "And they've got three dogs. Two small terriers and one tied up at the back. I'm sure that's a pit bull."

He said that the name of the couple was Hamner. "The door's always locked, they've no letter-box and you won't catch me going round the back. It's like Fort Knox up there."

On his way home from school Tom collected Maisie. She ran ahead, limping a bit because she had the change from her dinner money in one of her shoes.

PC Mick was standing on the opposite side of the lane. He waved to Maisie as she ran past, and beckoned Tom over.

"Look what I found in the road," he said.

Sickened, Tom gazed at the remains of the mutilated badger. It had been an animal the size of a small dog.

"They want us to think it was hit by a car," said Mick. "They've deliberately maimed this one before baiting it. And all for the sake of a bet." He shook his head.

"I'll catch them, Tom, make no mistake about that. But what I want to do to them wouldn't be allowed in law."

"An eye for an eye, a tooth for a tooth," thought Tom.

He remembered a TV programme he had seen, with young badgers poking their stripy noses out of a hole in a woodland bank and gambolling about in the moonlight.

The phrase "An eye for an eye, a tooth for a tooth" resounded in his head all the way home.

It had rained in the day, but the evening was hot and sultry. Mick came into the pub and ordered a long drink of lime juice and soda. He was wearing his jogging suit and trainers. He took his drink to a deserted corner of the room and opened a newspaper.

"But they won't come back," thought Tom. "Not after last night. They're probably back in Manchester or Rotherham by now."

He had not, of course, told Maisie about the badger. She would have cried herself to sleep over it. He had not told his mother or father either. He hugged it to himself, a dark, sickening secret.

"If only," he thought, "I could *do* something."

Why, after pretending to go to bed early, he dragged his clothes back on and left the house, he could not have explained to anyone. What he had in mind he did not really know. Perhaps he intended to smash the windows of Seth Hamner's house, or just scream out "murderer!" But something, or someone, was pulling him inexorably towards Gants Field.

Dark clouds were hanging heavy in the sky that night. The heat was almost unbearable. But when he reached Gants Field the moon showed itself, in stark contrast with the black, prehistoric shapes which seemed, in a sudden moment of terror, to be rearing up at him.

And then he saw it – a great dark shadow moving towards the house at the top of the hill. And, after an age of silence, the wind starting up and, in the wind, the screaming. Over and over again, half-demented, almost human.

★ ★ ★

Seth Hamner's wife had found his body, covered in blood and mud, at the bottom of the garden and she hardly recognized him at first.

The injuries, Tom learned later, were identical to those inflicted on the badger. The pit bull terrier was still on its chain and the killer was never found. Tom thought of telling PC Mick about the dark shadow, but did not want to look foolish.

There was the footprint, though, in the spongy soil of Gants Field. A huge, clawed footprint, as if made by some prehistoric animal, or a giant badger.

Even Mick did not know what to make of that.

Mister Glove

I was walking through the antiques arcade in Islington, on my way to my first job, when something caught my eye in a shop window. A Mr Punch doll of the old-fashioned type, wearing a dark red velvet military hat, with tassels and gold brocade. The smile on its face was an evil smile and its eyes seemed to swivel, protuberant in their sockets, as it glared at me.

With a freezing of the blood I recognized it instantly. Mister Glove. And from that day I avoided the arcade and walked to work on the street outside, even in the worst of summer rains, when the cigarette packets and the chocolate wrappers and all the flotsam and jetsam of city life rose up from the gutters on a tide of dark water.

Years before, when still a child and holidaying with my father and mother and sister at the seaside, I had come across a Punch and Judy show. Lorna, my sister, had spotted it first. The donkey I had been stroking, with the name "Speedy" on its harness, was gazing humbly out to sea, and waiting for its twentieth rider that day. Nearby, Maybell, Jezebel and Petunia snorted a little and shook their colourful reins and bells, making jingle-jangle noises.

"Having a ride?" asked the donkey-woman and I shook my head, feeling, I remember, rather offended. Donkeys were for small children, after all, and I was nearly thirteen. I wondered whether to tell the woman about my horse-riding lessons.

Then I saw Lorna waving madly at me. She was with a crowd of children, further down the beach, and they were clustered round a gaily-painted red-and-white-striped booth. The donkey-woman sniffed.

"Flippin' Punch and Judy. Gets in the way of my rides, he does."

I ran over to Lorna. The children round the booth were jumping up and down and yelling,

22

"LOOK OUT!" to Mr Punch as a Ghost – in the form of a grey sheet with eyes – rose up behind him.

"WAAH!" cried the Ghost, and the children shouted as Mr Punch collapsed in fright.

"You're a bit old for this sort of thing," I said, remembering the donkeys.

"Sssh," whispered Lorna. "It's good."

"I'VE KILLED MR PUNCH," announced the Ghost. Mr Punch poked his nose up at the children.

"OH NO YOU HAVEN'T!" they cried.

"OH YES I HAVE!" cried back the Ghost, and the children screamed with delight as Mr Punch picked up a stick and hit the Ghost, making WAAAH! noises of his own. A Clown popped up his head and carried a tin onto the stage.

"How many people are behind there?" I whispered.

"Just one, of course," said my sister

"But there are three dolls on at once, all moving," I said. "How could one person do that?"

"Perhaps he has an assistant," replied Lorna. But as the show ended, and the children were clapping and cheering the victorious Mr Punch, only one man came from behind the booth, holding out a bottle for money. He had a shock of wavy black hair, and bushy eyebrows, and wore a silk scarf knotted round his neck, gipsy fashion. The children swarmed round the man, looking at the puppets. One small boy tried to run off with the Crocodile.

"You come back here," shouted the man, "or I'll make you into sausages!"

Lorna picked up a puppet which had fallen into the sand. It was the figure of a Judge with wig, spectacles, a beaked nose and huge yellow teeth.

"That one's a bit different," said the man. "I put that one on my head, see."

He held Mr Punch in his right hand and the Policeman in his left. The Judge fitted like a cap on his head and he turned it from one to the other.

"So that's how you did it," cried Lorna. "How clever!"

I picked up the Judy puppet. She glared back at me with bulging eyes. She had a huge, hooked nose, identical to Mr Punch's, and her hair, sprouting underneath the checked cotton mob-cap, seemed to be made of some kind of matted grey fur. I had never seen anything so ugly in my life.

24

"Do you make these puppets yourself?" asked Lorna.

"All of them," said the man. "That's the part I like best. Making the puppets."

He wrapped the dolls carefully in dusters, placing them in a battered suitcase. Most of the children had wandered away to the ice-cream van near the car park.

"The donkey-woman hates me," said the man. "But I get on well with Shorty over there. It makes the kids thirsty, all that yelling. He sells twice as much ice cream when I'm around."

We watched as he unhooked the painted canvas from round the booth. He unslatted the booth into three pieces and put them on a trolley.

"I wheel everything on this trolley. I live just along there."

He pointed to the car park.

"In the caravan?" said Lorna. "We wondered who that belonged to."

The man picked up the Mr Punch doll, examining the peeling red paint on his nose and cheeks.

"Poor old fellow," he said. "He's had his day. I've nearly finished making a new one.

25

You can come and see him if you like. I'm the Professor, by the way."

I felt puzzled by the Professor. He seemed so outgoing and friendly, but there was something strange about him. How could any ordinary sort of person make dolls like these? I had seen Punch and Judy puppets before and they were never very pretty. But every one of the Professor's dolls had a sort of grotesqueness about it. Even the Clown had a peculiar look.

Lorna, I saw, was following the Professor to his caravan. I was not at all sure that this was a safe thing to do, and determined that I would only stand on the steps and look inside. There were plenty of people on the beach and in the car park, all within shouting distance. I had to keep my eye on Lorna. Although a year older than me, she sometimes behaved like a child of ten.

A small, black cat with yellow eyes was perched on the steps of the Professor's caravan. The caravan was on the far side of the car park and nearby the land dropped steeply to the beach.

"I practise the show down there sometimes, late at night, when there's no one about," he said.

I thought this sounded rather spooky.

26

"Have you ever been washed out to sea?" asked Lorna

"I nearly was once," he laughed.

The air which came from inside the caravan had a fusty smell. From the doorway I could see that the bed was pulled out from the wall and scraps of material and fur were strewn all over it.

Lorna had climbed into the room and was pointing to a large container in the sink partition.

"Plaster of Paris," said the Professor. "For making moulds. The dolls have hollow heads, you see. Solid wood's no good when you're doing ten shows a day. Exhausts you."

My eyes slowly became accustomed to the gloom inside the caravan. From all directions, other eyes were watching me. The room was full of puppets.

"This is the latest," said the Professor. "I've nearly finished him."

He held up a hump-backed Mr Punch doll, with a hooked nose and chin and furrowed brow. Although the puppet was grinning, its expression was unpleasant, almost sinister.

"Could I hold him?" asked Lorna

She put her thumb in one arm and her middle finger inside the hollow head of the doll.

"Put your fourth and fifth fingers inside the other arm," said the Professor, "and wiggle him about. Now, see if you can pick up this stick."

Laughing, Lorna manoeuvred the velvet-clad arms of the doll round the stick. She came towards me in the doorway and began to tap my arm with it. The tapping became more and more insistent.

"Look out!" I cried. "You're hurting me."

My sister dropped the doll and the Professor picked it up and dusted it down.

"Naughty boy," he said, and his voice was almost a caress. "Eager to get to work, are you?"

He turned to us.

"When I was a young lad, much younger than you, my elder brother threw a leather glove into my lap. It lay there like a spider. It seemed to have a life of its own. 'That's Mister Glove,' he said. 'Mister Glove's after you.'"

I stared at the shining eyes of the Professor, and at the shining eyes and grinning red mouth of the doll.

"Weird," I thought to myself. "Really weird."

It was my favourite word of the moment.

★ ★ ★

"The hat's unusual, isn't it?" said Lorna, as we walked back along the beach "I suppose it's the sort they wore in the old days. All the Mr Punch dolls I've ever seen had stripy caps with bells."

Suddenly she stopped, and shivered.

"Louise, I wish we hadn't said we'd help out with the show in the morning. I don't want to."

"It's your fault," I said crossly. "What did you have to agree for?"

She was silent for a moment, kicking up pebbles. Then she said quietly,

"It wasn't me hitting you with the stick, Louise. It was Mister Glove. He just wouldn't stop. I don't want to hold him in the booth tomorrow."

"I will then," I said. "Honestly, Lorn, you are a fairy."

But, remembering the expression on the puppet's face, I did not feel too happy about holding him either.

The next morning I could have laughed at my fears. The early mists were disappearing fast and the sea and every rock-pool glittered diamonds.

"Just smell that *air*," cried Lorna, as we ran

towards the part of the beach where the Professor, in a crisp cotton shirt, had already set up the booth and was hanging the Dog Toby, Joey the Clown, the Policeman, the Doctor, the Judge and the Hangman, together with a frying-pan and a string of sausages, on hooks round the side of it. Children, with their mothers and fathers, had already started to gather round.

"That part of the canvas is semi-transparent," explained the Professor. "I can see them, but they can't see me. Which of you is going to help me start the show?"

"Louise will," said Lorna quickly. "I'll go out front and watch."

"Take hold of Mister Glove, then, the way I showed your sister yesterday," said the Professor.

I did so, rather hesitantly.

"There's quite a crowd out there now. I'll go and tell them I've lost Mister Glove – Mr Punch to them, of course! Each time I say it, you pop his head up. When I turn round, drop him into this dip in the canvas. All right?"

I nodded. I tried not to look at the hump-backed doll, whose grin seemed wider than ever in the morning light.

"Good morning, children," called the Professor, stepping round in front of the booth. The children dutifully shouted "Good morning" back. Peeping through the open-work part of the canvas, I held tightly on to Mister Glove.

"An awful thing happened to me when I was coming here," the Professor was saying, "I don't really know how to tell you. You'll be so disappointed. Can you guess what happened? My suitcase fell open and I lost Mr Punch. How am I going to do a Punch and Judy show without Mr Punch?"

This was my cue for popping the head of the puppet over the rim of the stage but, try as I might, the puppet would not move. It seemed to be resisting me. I could feel my hands starting to sweat.

"Can you see him anywhere?"

I saw the Professor give an anxious glance over his shoulder.

"Will you shout if you see him?"

The children were silent. I made another attempt to propel the puppet towards the stage.

"Perhaps I'd better go and have a look." I heard the Professor say "Stay there a minute. Don't go away."

He joined me behind the canvas, looking rather cross.

"I couldn't help it," I whispered. "I can't move him."

"Never mind," said the Professor. "I'll carry on from here. You go and watch the show with your sister."

I went and knelt with Lorna at the back of the audience of children, who were now clapping at the sudden appearance of Mr Punch.

"What happened?" whispered Lorna. "I thought you were supposed to do that."

I mouthed "tell you later" as Mr Glove's strange voice, produced by the Professor with a swazzle in his mouth, began calling for Judy.

"He really is clever," whispered Lorna, as the scene progressed and Judy brought in the Baby. "Look at the way he's walking the Baby backwards and forwards across the stage."

We watched as Mr Glove picked up the Baby and cradled it in his arms, singing

> "O rest thee my darling
> Thy mother will come
> With a voice like a starling
> I wish she were dumb."

"He sounds different from the other Mr Punch," said Lorna. "I don't remember that bit. Look how he's hitting the Baby. Here comes Judy. Look how he's hitting her!"

The puppet seemed to have gone out of

control, flinging the Baby into the air and hitting Judy so hard that her head fell off. The children were jumping and shouting with glee, but I saw one or two of the parents exchanging glances. The Professor established some sort of control for the scene with the Policeman, but the Judge had his wig torn off and his spectacles broken. The Crocodile, after gobbling down the string of sausages, held firmly onto Mr Glove's nose for several minutes but the Doctor, who followed the Crocodile onto the stage, had the "nasty medicine" bottle forced down his throat and when the Hangman arrived with the gallows Mr Glove seemed to go mad again, swinging the black-coated figure round and round in his noose, crying "Look, I've caught a kipper!" and flinging him to the far side of the crowd.

When the Professor came out at the end of the show his hands were shaking. He did not bother to collect any money and shooed the children away as fast as he could. He did not seem to want to talk to us, either.

"Come on, Lorna," I said. "Let's go for a paddle. My feet are baking."

As we were splashing through the rockpools later that day, I felt my toes sink into something soft and furry. I leapt out of the pool with a scream.

"What is it?" cried Lorna, running towards me.

"There's something in there. An animal of some sort."

I felt rather sick. Lorna peered into the pool.

"Why, it's Toby," she cried. "The Professor's dog, Toby."

She pulled out the small animal with snapping jaws, which the Professor had made by joining two pieces of wood at one end and covering them with an old pair of fur slippers.

"There's something else in there, as well."

She dragged out Joey, the Clown doll, oozing sea water. One of its arms, and the back of its head, was missing.

"The Professor must have dropped them out of his suitcase," she said, shaking the water from Joey's ruffles.

"Unless they were pushed," I muttered.

"Don't be daft. We'd better take them back to him. Not that they'll be much use now."

We reached the corner of the car park to find the curtains at the caravan windows drawn and the door locked.

"Let's leave them outside. He's probably asleep," I whispered, but Lorna was already banging on the door. After a few moments the Professor came out in his dressing-gown, looking rather pale and dazed. When he saw us he rubbed the back of his head and sat down on the top step of the caravan.

"I was having a lie-down," he said. "How my head hurts. I must have sat up in my sleep and banged it on something. Do you want to come in?"

"It's OK," I said. "We have to get back to the hotel. We're going out this evening."

"We brought you these. We found them in a rockpool. You must have dropped them," chimed in Lorna.

The Professor gazed at the broken puppets without any interest. The small black cat which had been resting on the roof of the caravan stood up, arched its back, and climbed down to curl up on his knee.

"Is she your cat?" asked Lorna. "Isn't she pretty! What's her name?"

"I call her Malkin," said the Professor. "But that's not her real name. Only she knows what her real name is."

He scratched the cat's ear, looking far-away and thoughtful.

"Cats have little pockets underneath their ears, you know – that's where they keep their secrets. You can tell her your secrets. They'll be safe."

I wondered if the bang on the head had affected the Professor's brain a little. I wondered how a person could possibly sit up in bed and bang his head, but supposed there wasn't much space in the caravan. Then I thought about Mr Glove, and the expression of glee he had worn when knocking Judy's head off.

"Bye, Professor, we'll have to go," I said quickly. "Mum and Dad are taking us to see a play tonight. Come on, Lorna."

I could not help comparing the audience in the theatre with the audience at the Punch and Judy show. The children watching Punch and Judy had bounced up and down on the sand and called out in excitement. The audience in the plush seats, largely composed of elderly ladies, tittered politely from time to time and held their hands up to their faces to hide their yawns.

When other people yawn, I have to yawn, too. And the play, set in a large house in the Scottish highlands, was the most boring thing I had ever seen. The lady next to me, who had blue-rinsed hair and wore a black silk dress under her mackintosh, kept rustling chocolate papers. How I wished she would offer me one – we had missed our evening meal to get to the theatre on time. My tummy started to rumble, and when I leant forward in an effort to stop it another lady, behind me, tut-tutted. Suddenly I remembered a bag of mint lumps in the glove compartment of the car.

"You can't go to the car now, Louise," my father said, when the interval came at last. "It's getting dark out there. Let's all go and get a drink or an ice cream in the bar."

"The car park's only just across the road and Lorna can come with me," I said, but Lorna would not leave the theatre. She had her best open-toed sandals on.

"All right, I'll go by myself," I said.

I pocketed the car keys, glad to escape from the stifling atmosphere of the foyer even for a short time.

The wind cut through my dress as I crunched across the car park, but the evening sky was clear and bright. I retrieved the mint-lumps and re-locked the car door, gazing towards the far side of the car park where the Professor's caravan made a dark, humped shape, with no lights at any of the windows. As I went closer I saw the black cat crouched on the roof of the caravan, her eyes shining strangely in the moonlight.

I shivered a little, my own eyes drawn to the great, white face of the moon. I walked to the edge of the car park, where it dropped down to the beach. The tide was out, and the sands were bathed in a clear, white light. Something was bobbing about in the dark, distant waters. A piece of driftwood, perhaps – a large piece of driftwood. I almost fancied it to be a body, and had to remind myself that bodies do not float about in genteel seaside resorts, where ladies with blue-rinsed hair rustle chocolate wrappers.

I did not realize, at first, that the strange shape in the middle of the sand was the Punch and Judy booth. Then I remembered the Professor saying that he sometimes practised on the beach, in the evening, when there was no one else about. I tiptoed towards the booth, listening to the odd noises made by the Professor with his swazzle. The 'Punch and Judy' sign above the booth had been replaced by a notice, in old-fashioned letters, which read:

THE MISTER GLOVE SHOW.

Mister Glove, his velvet coat and silver buttons resplendent in the moonlight, was bowing and turning as if to Judy, but no other puppet was present on the stage. He held in his arms the Baby, which the Professor had made from a wooden peg, wrapped in a linen napkin.

"Hushabye, Hushabye," cooed Mister Glove, rocking and stroking the Baby. Then he screamed, "Naughty child – Judy! The child has got the stomach ache. Keep quiet, can't you? I won't have such a naughty child. Hold your tongue!"

I wondered if the Professor could see me, through the peep-hole. As I was in the shadows, I thought he probably could not. I decided to creep along by the break-water and surprise him. Mister Glove had started to strike the Baby against the side of the booth.

"There! There! There! How do you like that? Get along with you – nasty, naughty, crying child!"

The peg, in its linen wrapping, flew through the air. It just missed my head. I thought the Professor had done it on purpose, that he had seen me after all.

I tiptoed to the back of the booth, then stood still, staring.

The frying-pan and the string of sausages were hanging neatly on their hooks, on either side of the booth. The crocodile grinned from his corner, next to the nasty-medicine bottle and the tin with the Ghost inside. Apart from the moving shadow of Mister Glove there was no sign of any other puppet.

And the Professor was nowhere to be seen.

The Ordeal of Oliphant Beamish

It was cool in the Aquarium after the hot, noisy pavements, but the soles of Adam's feet were still sore and throbbing against his plastic flip-flops. He gazed longingly into the pool where huge carp, tench, goldfish, and other fish which he did not recognize, flicked their tails and glided effortlessly.

"Look at that orange and black one," said his younger brother Marty. "The shark's not in the pool, though."

"Well, of course it isn't," said Adam, scornfully. "*He'd* hardly be in there with a shark."

He pointed to a diver who, in mask and wet-suit, was feeding a jagged sliver of raw, red meat to one of the fish.

"Can we feed the diver?" called out Marty, for the benefit of a group of giggling people on the other side of the pool.

"Stop showing off," said Adam fiercely.

Other divers were lowering themselves into the water, offering fistfuls of meat to be sucked up by the fishes.

"Shall we give some steak to Elvis the Pelvis when we get back home?" asked Marty.

"Just you try it," said Adam, "and see what Mum has to say. He *is* her fish."

As the divers slid into the water, thousands of bubbles rose to the surface. Thousands more rustled and popped at the edge of the pool where the pure, bright water rushed in from a hidden underground pipe.

"Mandy's found a sea-enema," said Marty. "She's waiting for it to eat something."

They joined the end of the queue to the right of the pool, jostling their way through the dark passage, lined on either side with tanks of tropical fish.

"Hello, Oscar," said a man ahead of them, staring mournfully at a large fish which stared mournfully back, jaws moving up and down as if he might be contemplating breakfast.

"Why is he called a 'Red Oscar'? He's all

grey," said Marty, flattening his nose in imitation of the fish against the glass front of the tank.

His twin sister was still staring at the sea-anemone.

"It looks like macaroni," said Marty. "How many fish has it eaten?"

"None," replied Mandy, in great disappointment. "They just swim in and out again. I want to see the shark."

"Wait a minute," called Adam. "Look at this lion fish, Mandy. And those little turquoise fishes lit up from inside."

Mandy pretended not to hear him. She made her way to the end of the passage, where the rushing of water was loudest, and stared in fascination at the sand-coloured, streamlined body of the shark. The shark, from its resting place on the floor of the tank, stared ahead unblinkingly.

"It's not all that big," said Marty, joining her. "And the notice says it's a nurse-shark. Not even very dangerous."

The shark, except for the rapid movement of water through the slitted gills in its side, was perfectly still. Its eye was small, grey and uncanny. Gazing at the shark, Adam felt a deep chill creeping up his body, into his very bones.

It was the chill of some savage past, of the eerie darkness of the ocean.

Suddenly there was a scream, the sound of wet feet against stone, and a splashing of water.

"Quick!" he cried. "Someone's fallen into the pool!"

The people nearby stared at him in astonishment, protesting, as he pushed them aside, ducked under the cord at the far end of the corridor and turned back into the centre of the building. The divers were still feeding the fish in a graceful, leisurely fashion. People chattered unconcernedly at the side of the pool, in groups of two or three.

"Didn't you hear it?" shouted Adam to the twins, who had followed him. "The scream, the running footsteps and the splash?"

"And you tell me not to show off," said Marty, in disgust. "I'm going to find Mum and Dad."

Puzzled, Adam followed his brother and sister down the first flight of stone steps, past the drinking fountain with the carved lion's head. He did not see, propped above the second flight, a notice which said, in old-fashioned letters,

THERMAL WATER SWIMMING BATH 68 DEGREES.
MIXED BATHING. EVERFLOWING WATER.
CHARGES: SWIMMING 2^d BATHING 2^d TOWEL 1^d.

Perspiration stood out in beads on Dad's forehead. Cheryl, Adam's older sister, was looking bored.

"Wherever have you been?" said Mum. "I'm dying for a cup of tea."

They edged their way into a crowded café and were served the tea, in a large metal pot, and some rather stale éclairs. Adam lifted the teapot lid and watched three sodden teabags floating about in the murky water.

"Why don't you and Dad come and look at the Aquarium?" he said. "It's good. There's a shark in one of the tanks."

"They promised to take us to the funfair!" cried Marty.

"And to the amusement arcade," added Mandy.

The amusement arcade was next to the café and the noise was deafening. Mandy made straight for the Metal Claw, which came down within a hair's-breadth of the bracelet she wanted, and dropped her a boiled sweet instead.

"20p for a boiled sweet," said Mum in disgust.

"I'm going down to that shop on the Parade," said Cheryl. "I want to look at those jeans again."

"I'll come with you," said Adam quickly. "They've got some good badges there."

Once on the High Street he waved goodbye to Cheryl and made his way back to the Aquarium. He wanted another look at the shark.

The main door of the building was closed. Adam went into the adjoining souvenir shop.

"Sorry," said the girl at the counter, "but we shut the Aquarium at five-thirty." A customer handed her an ashtray and a local tea-towel.

"Couldn't I just go in until the shop closes?" pleaded Adam.

"Oh, all right," replied the girl. "You'll have to leave when I come to lock up, though."

Adam went through the side door of the shop and climbed the first flight of steps. At the top he saw a woman filling a cup at the stone fountain. He thought at first she must be in evening dress. The woman exclaimed loudly, and a man rushed in from a side door.

"Look, Herbert," cried the woman, pointing to her cup. "There's a fish in there. A red and turquoise fish."

Adam went up to them, hoping to catch a glimpse of the fish in the cup, but the man and woman took no notice of him. He might have been invisible.

The noise of rushing, bubbling water was

louder than ever. Adam traced the source of it, behind the door which the man had opened and up some back stairs. He found himself in a short passage which led directly to a small courtyard and the open air. He was face to face with a huge water-pipe, surrounded by a tunnel. The water, carried from the hills, perhaps, gushed and swished from the pipe in a restless torrent, finding its way eventually, Adam guessed, to the pool. He walked towards the more familiar corridor, staring in amazement. For instead of fish-tanks there were dressing-cubicles, and in the place where the shark had been a rather portly man, with a bright red face, was busy enveloping himself in a towel. Although Adam stirred, the man took no notice of him.

"Coo-ee," said a soft voice, and he turned to see a woman dressed in a most peculiar bathing-costume which had sleeves, frilly knickerbockers and a tiny skirt. She was wearing on her head a cap rather like the one Adam's mother put over her hair-rollers, when preparing for a night out.

"Coming for a dip? The water's lovely," said the woman.

"Think I'll just have my bath today," replied the man. "Rheumatism playing up, you know."

He followed the couple into the main part of the building, where he remembered the pool had been, and saw to his astonishment that someone had placed steps at one end of the pool and people were jumping into the water with flurries of bubbles far in excess of those caused by the divers. There were no divers to be seen now, and no fish, either. The people, thought Adam, in their uncomfortable, clinging costumes, were queerer than any fish.

"Why dress like that," he thought, "for a swim?"

One of the women, who actually had ruffles of lace stitched on to her bathing-dress, gave a cry.

"There's something down there in the water," she called out. "Something moving. I think it's alive."

"It's a fish!" cried someone else. "A large mirror carp, by the look of it. How on earth did a fish get into the water?"

Try as he might, Adam could see no fish. The women scrambled from the pool in consternation, whilst the braver of the men waded in to try to grasp the trespasser. Their hands, it seemed, would not close round it.

"Drat the thing," said the portly man, who

48

in the excitement of the moment had entered the water still wearing his towel. "It's got no substance at all. Must be a trick of the light."

Dripping and complaining, he made for his cubicle and a dry towel.

"Look what I've found," cried a small, fair woman, hurrying from the direction of the cubicle where the sea-anemone had been. "What do you suppose it *is*? The latest kind of massage sponge?"

The conversation was shattered by a sudden blood-curdling scream. The portly man, half of him covered with a dry towel and half with a wet one, ran in terror from his cubicle. His bare foot caught the corner of the wet towel and he skidded, banging his head on the side of the pool and falling into the water with a great splash and a fountain of bubbles.

Adam, horrified, rushed to the edge of the pool. He found himself gazing into depths illuminated by powerful underwater lamps which played red, green and golden on the backs of twisting, sliding fish. Except for the fish, he was quite alone. Above him, the pointed iron framework of the roof opened to chimney pots and the darkening splendour of a late August sky. The girl from the souvenir shop came in, rattling a bunch of keys rather obviously. "Seen everything yet?" she asked him.

"Yes . . . thank you . . . everything," said Adam in a dazed, dumbfounded way. He could still hear the water rushing from the underground pipes in the underground tunnel which was so old . . . nearly as old as the hills . . .

"Wherever have you been?" said Mum crossly, for the second time that day. "We've missed the first sitting, thanks to you."

The family were assembled in the front room of the b & b and, as usual when the family were all together, they had the room almost to themselves. One quiet, elderly lady, a resident guest for summer and winter, smiled at them from a corner. She had introduced herself at breakfast that morning as Miss Spriggs. She had lived, she said, all her life in the town and seen many changes. Adam desperately wanted to talk to her about the Aquarium.

"Oh yes, I remember it as a swimming pool," said Miss Spriggs. "I swam there myself, as a girl." Adam tried out, in his mind, how long ago that would have been.

"It's what is known as a thermal pool," she said. "The waters there are warmish and said to be very good for the health. It seems a pity to waste it on fish, in a way."

"Did they have hot baths, as well, when you were a girl?" asked Adam. "For people with rheumatism?"

"Yes," said Miss Spriggs, "and cubicles to change in. Those date back to the Victorian era. That's even before *my* time," she laughed, seeing his expression. "I've some photographs, if you'd like to see them."

"You can go for five minutes," said his mother. "Come down as soon as you hear that clock chime."

Adam was already halfway up the stairs . . .

Miss Spriggs's room was simply and neatly furnished. It was on the cool side of the house and smelt faintly of camphor and lavender wax.

"I'm afraid I have to keep this under the bed," she sighed, pulling out a large, leather-bound album. "There's nowhere else to put it."

The album was full of old sepia photographs, newspaper cuttings, even old concert programmes, beautifully coloured and designed.

"Here we are," she said at last. "The Thermal Pool in the 1880s . . . special treatments for rheumatic ailments, nerve troubles, digestive disorders and other complaints."

The pool in the picture, surrounded by bathers in striped, frilly costumes, was just as Adam had seen it. There were steps at the edge of the pool and the roof of the building was fitted with glass.

"I don't remember it then, of course," said Miss Spriggs, eyeing Adam over her bifocals, "but my Aunt Polly did. I particularly remember her telling me, as a girl, of an accident that happened there."

Adam waited, hardly daring to breathe.

"Aunt Polly used to visit the pool regularly with a business friend from Manchester. Oliphant Beamish, he was called. The name stuck in my mind, it was such a funny one. Mr Beamish suffered rather badly from rheumatics, I believe. Well, one day strange things started happening at the pool. People saw fish everywhere, but couldn't touch them. They seemed to be an illusion, some sort of trick of the water and light, Aunt Polly said. And Mr Beamish saw something in his dressing cubicle which made him rush out, screaming. He caught his head on the pool's edge and fell in. No one ever knew what frightened him so much, as the fall affected his memory and he was never able to tell them."

As Miss Spriggs chattered on, Adam's eyes

grew wider and wider. He almost missed the chime of the suppertime clock.

"What do you mean, you saw a ghost?" sniffed Mum.

"Anyway," said Marty, "you didn't *see* anything. You only *heard* it. You said you heard a scream, running footsteps and a splash."

"I saw the man later," said Adam, "when I went there on my own. He was running from the cubicle. He looked as if he'd seen a ghost."

"A ghost frightened of a ghost?" Mum sniffed again. "What sort of ghost would that be? Do you want vinegar or parsley sauce?"

"I saw ghosts of the past," said Adam, slowly. "Perhaps he saw a ghost of the future . . . "

"A ghost of the future, that's rich," laughed Dad, digging into his lamb chop. "We're all going to be haunted by little green men, are we?"

"Not our future, *his* future," said Adam.

He looked at the fish on his plate, seeing in his mind another fish with small, cold grey eyes and a body the colour of sand. He stared at the bubbles in his glass of lemonade which fizzled, rose to the surface, broke, fizzled, rose again. The pink, pulpy remains of the chop lay on his father's plate. He remembered the fish taking meat from the hands of the divers and thought over and over his conversation upstairs with Miss Spriggs.

"The most dreadful part of all," Miss Spriggs had told him, "was that when they pulled poor Mr Beamish from the pool to give him artificial respiration they found most of his big toe missing. Aunt Polly was there, and she swore to it. It wasn't trapped or anything. They never found the toe and Aunt Polly, who was not given to exaggeration, said it looked almost as if it had been bitten off. Mr Beamish was certainly cured of his rheumatism, though. He never complained again about *that*."

Tiberius and Tweet

"It's really too bad of Cynthia!" cried Miss Popplewell. "How can I look after a canary with Tibs in the house?"

Tiberius glared at her from the back of the armchair. He detested being called "Tibs".

"How long has your sister left the canary for?" asked Anita.

"A week." Miss Popplewell shook her head and a shower of hairpins fell to the floor. "For a whole week I have to keep Tiberius out of the back parlour. He won't like it. He won't like it at all."

Anita did not much like Tiberius. He was not the sort of cat one could pick up and cuddle and stroke. His long black and white fur had a permanent bristle, rather as if an electric current was being passed through it. She had never heard him purr, although he did make a tiny gurgling noise in his throat when he succeeded in upsetting Miss Popplewell.

Miss Popplewell was frequently upset. Anita, on her way to school in the morning, would often see her in tears over the lifeless, whiskery snout of some small mouse or shrew. Tiberius would be lurking on the roof of the coal-shed.

"We can't blame him, really," Miss Popplewell would shudder, pulling on her gardening gloves and disentangling the tiny corpse from the milk bottle. "He thinks he's doing me a favour. He can't go out and buy a box of chocolates, can he?"

Soon after the arrival of Tiberius, Miss Popplewell had turned vegetarian. Whilst she nibbled at cheese, salad and brown rice, Tiberius flourished on breast of chicken, flaky white codfish and sardines in tomato sauce.

"Grandad says you spoil him," said Anita. "He sent you these radishes. Could I look at the canary, do you think? What's his name?"

"Cynthia didn't bother to tell me," sniffed Miss Popplewell. "Didn't have time. You know my sister. Left no food for him, either. Lucky we have that corner shop. I'll just put Tiberius outside, or he'll try to squeeze through the parlour door."

With Tiberius protesting loudly from the street, Miss Popplewell led Anita into her dark back room, which was full of plastic flowers and smelt of moth-balls. A large wire cage had been placed on the table, and in it a small yellow bird preened his feathers and warbled prettily.

"Is it a he or a she?" asked Anita, staring.

"A he, I think," replied Miss Popplewell. "She-canaries don't sing, for some reason. Too much on their minds, I suppose, with laying eggs. Look how unsafe the catch is."

"He sings beautifully," said Anita. "You ought to call him 'Tweet'."

The bird surveyed his reflection in a tiny mirror which hung from the cage, tapped his beak and trilled in agreement.

Anita ran to tell her grandfather about Tweet, but Grandad only tapped the stem of his pipe on the table. He was not very fond of birds. They ate his peas and Brussels sprouts and dug up his marigold seeds as soon as he planted them.

"If the birds don't get my seeds," he said, "that wretched cat scrabbles them up chasing after the birds. Miss Popplewell should do a bit of gardening herself, then she'd know."

"Have you put the beans in yet?" asked Anita. "You said I could help."

"I've made the sticks ready," said Grandad. "And there's something you could do which would help me a lot."

He went into the kitchen and pulled out a drawer full of bottle-tops and silver tinfoil dishes which had once held pies.

Anita followed him into the kitchen.

"Miss Popplewell asked me to remind you about the water tank," she said.

"What about it?" replied Grandad. "It's useful under the wall there, when I can't be bothered to get the hose out."

"She says it's dangerous. She says if you can't move it, will you put a cover on it?"

"I might," said Grandad, "and I might not. Now, I want you to take these bits of tinfoil and thread them together with string . . . like this . . . so that they rattle together."

"Are you going to tie them on the bean-sticks?" asked Anita.

"That's right. They'll keep the birds at bay when the wind's blowing."

"Here's a nice big piece," said Anita. "I could cut a shape out of this."

"Do what you like," said Grandad, "as long as they rattle."

The next day was Saturday, sunny and fine. Anita dressed quickly and ran up the hill to say good morning to Tweet. She met Miss Popplewell at her cottage door in a state of near hysteria.

"Quickly, do something!" shrieked Miss Popplewell. "Get it off him, get it off!"

Tiberius, on the doormat, was bristling even more than usual and his yellow eyes were starting to bulge. A slim grey slow-worm, yanked mercilessly by the cat from its hole in the wall, had wrapped itself round his neck and was pulling tighter and tighter. Anita picked up a stick and tried to loosen the slow-worm. Miss Popplewell ran in panic for her gardening gloves. Tiberius, with a demoniac screech, twisted his head sideways and bit the slow-worm. In a flash the snake uncoiled itself and disappeared, minus tail, down a nearby drain.

"I can't take much more of this butchery," said Miss Popplewell. She tottered into the house and collapsed on the sofa.

"He's doing it on purpose, just because I won't let him go into the back room. Last night he brought in a bat. It was only a baby, and it lay on the hearthrug, panting in terror."

"Shall I make you a cup of tea?" asked Anita. She felt sorry for Miss Popplewell, and almost wished the slow-worm had strangled Tiberius.

"I haven't time, dear. I'm expecting visitors. They're due to arrive at eleven o'clock. Mr James is giving us a harp recital, and I'm preparing a vegetarian lunch. Of course I'm all behind, with one thing and another, and right out of brown bread."

"I can bring you some," said Anita. "I'm going down for Grandad's steak-and-kidney pie."

"Would you, dear . . . so kind," said Miss Popplewell, flinching a little at the mention of kidney. "Now let me just check the yoghurt situation."

"Will none of your visitors eat meat?" asked Anita.

"Oh no." Miss Popplewell sounded quite shocked. "We all hold the same views about it. To tell you the truth, Anita, I feel quite sick sometimes when I'm preparing food for Tibs."

Anita looked at Tiberius, who licked his lips and stared at his mistress with yellow, malevolent eyes.

"I can't see him eating nut cutlets," she said. She was climbing the hill, clutching Grandad's pie, still warm from the bakery, when a large blue car followed by a small white car drew up outside Miss Popplewell's cottage. Miss Popplewell ran to greet the man who had climbed out of the blue car and was edging from it a huge, unwieldy instrument wrapped in a cloth. Two women, of about the same age as Miss Popplewell, ran from the white car, laughing shrilly.

"Here's the bread," said Anita. "Is that the harp, Miss Popplewell?"

"Yes, dear – come inside and have a look at it."

"Oh, what a darling cat!" cried one of the women, stooping. Tiberius spat and put out his claws. He viewed the looming, cloth-covered shape with great suspicion, and disappeared under the car to plan tactics. He was furious with his mistress, first for harbouring a bird in a cage, and then for planning a party without his permission. To hear tinkling laughter, oohs and aahs of delight, made Tiberius beside himself with rage. He narrowed his eyes and flexed his claws, determined to spoil the fun.

Inside the cottage, Anita gazed in awe as Mr James unwrapped the splendid, shining harp. When he ran his fingers across the strings the sound that rippled across the room, like a thousand heavenly waterfalls, was so clear and cold and sweet it made her backbone quiver.

Outside, Tiberius felt his backbone quiver, not in pleasure but in fury at the unearthly sound. He started to make unearthly sounds of his own, practised in alleys and on roof-tops throughout black, moonless nights.

"Stop it, Tibs. Stop it!" cried poor Miss Popplewell from the window. The cat continued on its caterwauling way.

With the recital ruined, Miss Popplewell tried to interest her friends in lunch, although it was barely half past eleven. Anita helped her to carry dishes of spiced rice and fried bananas into the living room, where her guests sat round with trays.

"Have you a bird, Hester?" asked a dark-haired woman with large teeth. "I thought I heard a bird singing."

"In the back room," replied Miss Popplewell. "I keep him out of harm's way in there."

"I do know what you mean," said the woman, rubbing the hand which had been clawed by Tiberius. "I've never known such a monster. Can I have a peep at the birdie?"

Tiberius who, when Mr James carried the harp back to the car, had crept through the door and hidden under the table, curled his lip

62

with pride. No one had ever actually called him a monster before. When the dark-haired woman came out of the parlour, leaving the door slightly open, he could hardly believe his luck . . .

"More rice, Joan?" asked Miss Popplewell. "Anita – you have some. It's nutritional. This little girl eats meat," she said, turning to her friends, "but we're winning her over, I think."

The dark-haired woman's fork clattered to the floor.

"Hester," she gasped, her teeth bared like tombstones. "Hester . . . "

She was staring in the direction of the back room. Framed in the doorway stood Tiberius, his fur bristling in a ghastly halo. Before him lay a pitiful bundle of still, yellow feathers. The whole company stared in frozen, disbelieving horror. Tiberius glanced at a plate of carrot mousse in withering contempt and leisurely, deliberately, picked up the bundle of feathers and crunched it. Miss Popplewell moaned and fell to the floor in a faint. As her friends rushed towards her, Anita rushed towards Tiberius, who leapt through the window with a cry of triumph. Sadly, she picked up what was left of Tweet.

★ ★ ★

"It's a bad business," said Grandad. "Know what I'd do if he was my cat." He opened the oven door and put in the steak-and-kidney pie. "What are you having to eat?"

"I'm not hungry," sighed Anita. "I had something to eat at Miss Popplewell's."

"Daft of her to get upset like that," said Grandad. "What's she doing now?"

"Her friends have taken her out for a car-ride. I think I'll go and bury Tweet in the garden."

"We'll make a start on the beansticks when I've had this pie," said Grandad.

Anita took the remains of the feathers to the very bottom of the garden, where it met the wood. She wrapped them in long grass and hid them under brambles, well away from the ants' nests. As she pulled down the brambles, trying not to get pricked, something bright and silver flashed past her head. She thought she must have imagined it.

Grandad had arranged sticks from the wood in a double row over the bean-patch. After dinner, he carried out an armful of the tinfoil shapes and they tied them with string to the tops of the sticks.

"You made a good job of these," he said. "We've an artist in the family."

"They're supposed to be canaries," said Anita.

"I thought they were seagulls," said her grandfather.

He tramped over to the water tank and peered at the round mosquito larvae which rode up and down in the dark water. He felt the crumbling wall above the tank with his elbow.

"Stone loose," he said. "No hurry, though."

Anita was staring up at Miss Popplewell's clothes-line, where tiny bluetits hung and pecked at a bag of peanuts. A small, silvery bird, almost transparent, was flying amongst the bluetits.

"I've never seen one like that, Grandad, have you?" she said.

"Never seen a bluetit?" said Grandad.

Tiberius was aware of the song of the bluetits, but even he had experienced enough excitement for one day. Well pleased with his morning's work, he decided to take a nap and hear again, in his dreams, Miss Popplewell's scream when he bit the tail off the slow-worm, her sighing moan as he gobbled up Tweet.

Flies buzzed and the afternoon sun slanted in through the window. Tiberius, who hated sunshine, made his way into the cool parlour. The door of the room had been left open and the door of the birdcage swung on its hinges. He curled himself up beside a plastic Madonna Lily, sighed contentedly, and was soon deep in dreams of terror and bloodlust . . .

So slept Tiberius, flexing his claws and twitching his tail, as the sun turned red and dropped behind the chimney-pots. A fresh breeze started up, the light in the room was dimming, but a strange, celestial glow was coming from the cage. Tiberius awoke, puzzled, to the sound of exquisite birdsong. It started softly, gradually filling every corner of the room. The pure, sweet sound was torture to Tiberius. He shifted his position several times, uneasily, and made his way to the kitchen in as nonchalant a manner as he could muster. The singing followed him, growing sweeter and purer by the minute as a ghostly canary flew from the cage and out of the parlour, flapping its transparent, silvery wings.

Tiberius howled. He ran into the garden and crouched under a clump of peonies, trembling and straining his ears. He heard the murmuring of collar-doves on the roof, the staccato warning of a blackbird, but the ghostly birdsong had not, it seemed, followed him into the garden. After an hour he began to relax and wonder what had happened to Miss Popplewell. His limbs ached and his tummy rumbled. Night was falling, but still she had not returned. Tiberius crept through the dusky garden jungle a frightened shadow of his former self, prompted to hunt by hunger for the first time in his life. At a sudden movement in the nettle-patch he stiffened, listening intently for the sound of a mouse or shrew rooting in the undergrowth. Some of the old feelings returned to him, but even as he poised to pounce, hindquarters wobbling slightly, there was a furious flapping of tiny, luminous wings above his head. Tiberius leapt in terror on to the garden wall. Beneath him rose a myriad of silver, tinkling tinfoil birds. Distraught, he lost his footing. A piece of the wall fell away and he dropped down, with a splash, into the water tank.

"What was that noise?" called Anita, who was in her pyjamas, watching television.

"I dropped a saucepan into the washing-up water," replied her grandfather, drawing the kitchen curtains.

Tiberius was floating . . . up and up into the evening sky, past the chimneys, now almost level with the top of the birch tree. It was a pleasant sensation. He could see, far below, Miss Popplewell weeping by the water tank. The silly woman was always weeping about something.

There was a rustle in the branches of the birch and he automatically tried to stiffen, but his body felt unreal, wispy, lacking in substance. A sparrow hopped out of the tree and flew away.

"Never mind," thought Tiberius, "I don't really care any more. It's such a glorious feeling . . ."

Something seemed to be sprouting at the back of him. It felt a bit like a pair of wings. He opened his mouth to sing like a heavenly canary, but the sound that issued forth was of all the devils in Hell.

Jem Crenna's Tune

"This is more like it," said Mrs Williams, as the car pulled into the harbour. "A truly unspoilt Cornish fishing village. Not like that other place. Polystyrene pixies, indeed!"

"The Harbour Guest House shouldn't be too difficult to find," said Mr Williams. "On the other hand they could all be called 'Harbour Guest House'."

He wound down the window of the car and called to a boy who was throwing sticks for a terrier with one ear.

"Could you direct me to Mrs Vincent's?" he asked.

The boy looked keenly at Mr and Mrs Williams and then at Christopher, who was huddled quietly in the back of the car with an assortment of bags and empty picnic boxes. The boy had a tanned skin and dark, penetrating eyes. He wore denim jeans, frayed just below the knee and a necklace of sea-shells. His feet were bare.

"Do you go to the far side of the harbour. That be Mrs Vincent's place," he said, in a quiet Cornish lilt.

The dog, who apart from his missing ear was a picture of canine health, barked excitedly, eager to return to his game. Mr Williams thanked the boy, who watched them drive to the opposite side of the harbour.

The guest house was at the end of a row of white-painted cottages with black shutters at the windows. Mrs Vincent rushed out to greet them. She was a large lady with dark, bushy hair and she wore spectacles attached to a long, gold chain. She had an air of noticing everything, without looking directly at anything.

"It's getting late. I'd just about been and given you up. This way," she said, leading Christopher up a narrow staircase to a small room with a low ceiling, wooden beams and a seat with a window which, to his delight, gave a fine view of the harbour. The tide was out, leaving fishing boats marooned in the soft mud.

"Perhaps this air will put some colour into his cheeks," said Mrs Vincent the next morning, staring at the dish of bacon and eggs she was putting on the table. "From the town, are you?"

"Yes, we live in London," said Mrs Williams. "And we have to go into town this morning, unfortunately – some business at the bank. As far as Wadebridge, anyway. Do you want to come with us, Christopher, or to stay here by yourself?"

"I'll stay," said Christopher, welcoming a morning of unexpected freedom. "I want to look at the fishing boats."

"Bit late for that," said Mrs Vincent. "Load up early, they do. Lovely weather for April, though. You enjoy yourself. If you don't want that bacon, the cat's a bit hungry this morning."

There was still one fishing trawler moored to the quay side and several rowing boats bobbing up and down in the water. One had a large, yellow-beaked gull at the helm, motionless as a figurehead. The tide was well in now and

Christopher sniffed the salty air, feeling for the first time that he really was by the sea.

He crossed to the harbour wall and peered over. Another fishing boat was moored to the right of steps which led to the water and the boy he had seen the evening before was squatting halfway down. Christopher watched, fascinated, as the boy drew from the water a long line with a wriggling brown crab at the end of it. He pulled in the line, wrenched off the crab and threw it into a plastic bowl. Christopher saw that attached to the line were several limpets, bait for crabs. He moved closer and peered into the bowl at the seething mass of crab, out of their element, slowly drowning in oxygen. He felt rather sorry for the crabs.

The boy leant forward and poured a jar of water over them. One of the crabs reached for him with its pincer and the boy laughed, lifting the crab with several others clinging to it.

"You can have her tonight, with sauce on," he said, indicating with his elbow an inn and restaurant overlooking the harbour.

"No need to look like that. If you were down there, under the water, she'd be eating you."

The one-eared terrier whined from the bottom of the fishing boat.

"No good at all for round here," said the boy. "Hates the water. Won't go near it."

"How did he lose his ear?" asked Christopher.

"How do you think?" said the boy, poking the crabs again.

He seemed to be laughing silently at Christopher, somewhere inside himself.

"I'll be dropping these off and going for a walk now. Want to come?"

After some argument with the owner of the Galley Inn over the price of the crabs, the boy led Christopher up steps away from the harbour and along a lane by the bottom of a golf course. They came to a high-up, asphalted area, with seats positioned to face the sea.

"What's that stone?" asked Christopher. "Is it a war memorial?"

"It's a memorial of sorts," said the boy. "Not war, though."

The grey slab had a picture of an old-fashioned sailing ship etched into it. Christopher read the inscription below:

"SACRED to the memory of 20 persons here interred, who were drowned in the wreck of the ship ARIEL, April 23rd, 1855. Erected by one of the survivors."

There followed a list of twenty names, with occupations.

"That's my name," said the boy suddenly, pointing to the lettering:

JEM CRENNA, CABIN BOY

"Your name?" asked Christopher, astonished. "Was he an ancestor of yours, then?"

The boy shrugged. "Maybe. That ship hit the Lyre Rock, out on the headland there. She followed a light, but it was the wrong light. Haven't you heard of the wreckers, then? They lured ships onto the rocks and looted the cargo."

Christopher followed the boy out into open country, burgeoning with yellow gorse bushes and tiny clumps of primroses in the grass. The land to their right fell sharply away to the sea. The dog barked excitedly and raced down a path, into the undergrowth.

"Follow him," said the boy and Christopher did so, the branches and brambles tugging at his clothes.

"What's that building hidden away in the wood?" he asked suddenly. "Is it an old lookout shelter?"

"That's right," said the boy. "Used to have guns pointing out to sea there."

It was dank and musty inside the shelter, but

as Christopher's eyes became accustomed to the half-light he saw some kind of bench, or table, with glass bottles, coins and pieces of wood on it.

"I pick them up on the beach," said the boy. "Nothing of value. Not like in the old days. Barrels of brandy they had then. Bales of silk. Beat them over the head for it, they would. Chop off their hands while they was clinging to the rocks."

Christopher shivered. He had heard tales of the wreckers, too. Jem leaned towards him, his voice low and husky.

"There are some say that when an inshore wind blows, and the evening mists are falling, a great black ship appears. She follows a light in the mist, a faint, bobbing light, but it is no help to her. The ship moves slowly, ever forward, towards the great Lyre Rock. There is a mighty crash, the sound of splintering wood, and voices crying out in terror. Then the wreckers come."

He moved away from Christopher, picking up a piece of hollow wood with holes drilled into it, and said in a matter-of-fact voice, "When a ship gets wrecked, the sails and rigging go first. The hull gets eaten by seaworms. Then it gets covered in silt. Preserves the contents, see? This pipe, now – fifty per cent seawater when I found her. Soaked her for a month in fresh."

"Does it play?" asked Christopher.

His mouth felt dry and his voice came out in a whisper.

"Oh, she plays." said the boy

He looked at Christopher, his eyes fathomless and dark with a hint of laughter in them.

"When the time is right, she plays."

They went out into the sunlight and walked for a mile between gorse bushes, as far as the jutting headland. Great black rocks loomed menacingly from the sea. Even in the midday heat, with the sky and sea a calm, unsullied blue, Christopher shivered. He looked at his watch.

"Nearly one o'clock," he said. "My mum and dad will be wondering what's happened to me. I'm supposed to be meeting them at the inn!"

"What a quaint place. I like the lobster pots round the light-bulbs," said Mrs Williams. "I think I'll try the crab salad. What about you, Christopher?"

"Not crab," said Christopher. "I don't like crab."

"How do you know? You've never tried it," said his mother.

"I'll just have the Ploughman's. I don't feel very hungry," said Christopher.

"What about shrimps?" said his mother. "Or local lemon sole? You must have seafood in a fishing village."

"Let the boy choose for himself," said Mr Williams. "Ploughman's it is. All right, Christopher? Bread, cheese and Branston pickle?"

The bread roll was small and the piece of cheese enormous. Christopher felt it settling solidly inside him. Afterwards they went out into the sunshine and his mother bought him a Cornish ice cream. He ate it on a seat overlooking the harbour, the sun beating against his head. A small industrial craft, a dredger, was lowering its metal claw into the water, clasping a load of soft black mud and disgorging it on deck.

"How about a ride in the car this afternoon?" said Mrs Williams. "We could take a look at King Arthur's castle."

"I don't think Christopher wants to take a look at anything," said Mr Williams. "Come on – you look dreadful. Back to the guest house with you."

Christopher lay in the darkened room, his hands tingling with dehydration. It was almost worth being sick to feel better for five minutes or so. Sounds of the harbour came to him and the sudden scream of gulls, raucous and menacing. The bed kept rocking to and fro like a ship and great black cliffs loomed in his mind. He saw rotting hulls of ships embalmed in seaweed, glittering with fish like tiny jewels. He saw a grinning figurehead with limpets where the eyes should be, and crabs milling round something at the bottom of the ocean.

There was a knock at the door and Mrs Vincent came in with a bottle of Milk of Magnesia.

"How are you, dear? Doctor says to try this and keep you on boiled water for a few hours. Oh dear, been sick again, have you? There's this bug going round, they've had it next door. Only twenty-four hours. Still, that's bad enough when you're on holiday. Been feeling bad all day, have you?"

"I felt all right this morning," whispered Christopher. "Until I ate the cheese. I went for a walk this morning. As far as the headland. I went with the boy with the dog."

"Jem Crenna?" said Mrs Vincent sharply, looking at the Magnesia bottle. "You don't want to bother with the likes of him."

"Is it true that wreckers used to live here in the old days?"

"No wreckers here," said Mrs Vincent. "No, indeed. They came from inland, mostly. What's he been telling you then?"

"He showed me a stone," said Christopher, "with the names of shipwrecked people on it."

"That wasn't wreckers," said Mrs Vincent. "Saved, most of the crew were, by local people. Some of them died doing it. Full of tales and mischief is Jem Crenna. Don't you listen to him. Now, you just take this, dear. If you're feeling better later I'll bring you up some cream crackers."

Christopher lay half awake, half dreaming for the rest of that day and most of the next, and slowly his stomach settled.

The weather had changed, with a strong breeze blowing, and he felt well enough by the evening to go with his parents to the Galley Inn.

The sound of music and clapping was coming from the saloon bar. Jem was sitting high on a table, playing "The Sailor's Hornpipe". Then he began to sing, in a high, raw, grating voice, a ditty about life at sea. The song was all about maggots in water bottles and rats chewing sailors' toenails as they lay asleep in their bunks. He waved in Christopher's direction.

"What a dreadful boy," said Mrs Williams. "He's not waving at me, I hope. I think I'll go into the other bar. Are you coming, Leonard? Christopher?"

His parents moved into the next room, but Christopher lingered. Jem Crenna finished his song and sauntered over to him.

"The pipe plays very well," said Christopher. "I don't believe it was from the sea at all."

"Suit yourself," said Jem.

"You like being mysterious," said Christopher. "Mrs Vincent says so."

"Does she now?" said Jem. "Been talking about me then, have you?"

"You said you'd play the pipe at the right time," said Christopher "Is this the right time?"

"Now's the time. But not the place," said Jem.

The dog ran into the room and out again.

"I'm going for a walk. Are you coming then?"

The walk along the tops of the cliffs, to the headland, seemed much longer with the wind blowing in from the Atlantic. Christopher felt cold with only a T-shirt under his jacket and his feet seemed to be dragging him back instead of helping him go forward. He still felt weak from lack of food, and the effort of climbing up and down steep paths, after nearly two days in bed, exhausted him. Not for anything would he tell Jem of his tiredness, or of his sickness bout. Jem would despise him for it. He reached the jutting promontory almost panting. The sun was dipping in the sky and the wind lashed the waves below them against huge rocks.

"There's a path down," said Jem, and Christopher followed him, his trainers gripping the smooth, worn stones.

They descended into a cove. Granite cliffs rose high to the sides of them and from the shelves of the cliffs seabirds made their last wild cries of the day. A thin waterfall trickled down one cliff, and underfoot the boulders were slippery from dark brown seaweed and the incoming tide. Christopher, sick with foreboding, noted every detail clearly, from the tiny snails nestled protectively in a crack in the granite to the jutting edge of the headland, like carious teeth. There were two rocks opposite, and further out to sea loomed the terrible-looking rock, the Lyre Rock, which had dashed ships to pieces like so many matchstick toys. How near the drowning people would be, he thought, and how impossible to save them.

Jem's dark eyes regarded him impassively. He crouched on a boulder, as if unaware of the ever-encroaching water, and started to play a jig. He played slowly at first, then faster, as if his life depended on it. He seemed to be playing despite the wind and waves, despite the falling mist and the evil, jagged rock, like an island in the half-light. The dog whined and pawed the water, his hackles rising. Jem's face became older, more determined, more set in its expression.

Behind him rose a monstrous apparition, a great, dark ship with sails unfurled heading inexorably, wave upon wave, towards a ghostly light which hovered in the distance, pointing towards the jagged rock. There was a sickening crash, the noise of shattering wood, and voices sobbing and wailing. Tiny black figures were bobbing in the water, clinging to bits of driftwood, grasping in vain at the slippery granite. The light from the headland was getting nearer. There was the sound of men's voices, the rattling of chains, the sudden glint of moonlight on a raised axe.

Christopher closed his eyes and screamed. He opened them to find the horizon clear and Jem looking at him, a strange mixture of amusement and triumph on his face. The dog had stopped whining and was worrying a piece of driftwood.

"I told you he didn't like the water," said Jem. "Here, you have a go."

He offered the pipe to Christopher.

"Play," said Jem.

Christopher put the pipe to his lips and blew three times. A strange, wailing sound came from it. Trembling, he gazed towards the water. He saw the rocks, immobile against a reddening sky. Nothing but waves moved on the ocean, and overhead the wind blew gently at a scudding armada of cloud.

Horrorgram

It was hot and stuffy inside the coach and the air smelt of smoke and stale tobacco. The windows were grimed with weeks of dirt – outside dirt, which did not shift when you rubbed them. They did not open, either. Overhead were knobs marked "air ventilators", but Ruthie did not dare to use them. Only ten miles from Manchester, and already her stomach was starting to heave.

"Hey, Ruthie, where d'you get that ring?"

Lisa's voice rose over the hubbub.

Lisa had insisted that Ruthie sit with her, right above the wheel of the coach, as she did whenever there was a school trip anywhere.

"The ring," demanded Lisa, her strong brown fingers closing over Ruthie's pale ones. "Where d'you get it?"

Ruthie's heart sank. She knew she should not have worn the ring – the silver ring with the little mother-of-pearl hearts on it.

"It came out of a cracker last Christmas," she lied.

"Some cracker!" said Lisa.

She had already pulled the ring off Ruthie's finger. It only fitted her own little one.

"Let me wear it today. I'll give it back later."

Ruthie knew she would not, that Lisa had taken the ring for herself, just as she had snatched Ruthie's sandwiches and shared them with Bonk and Harry Chan. Not that Ruthie cared about the sandwiches, or the bar of chocolate and the fruit cake, all carefully packed by her mum.

The faintly sulphurous smell of egg still lingered in the air, as the coach gave a particularly nasty lurch.

"I can't be sick in here," she thought in panic. "Not in front of everyone."

Miss O'Grady was in the front, chatting to the deputy teacher, her bright chestnut curls lifted by a tiny current of air which found its way through the rattling, badly-fitting door.

Now and then she would call to form 4B to look at the sheep and the fields of horses. When, after about an hour and a half, they drove between the towering limestone crags of Warlock Bath and into the coach park, Ruthie scrambled out with the others, breathing in lungfuls of clear, fresh air. At least she hadn't been sick.

The wells in the coach-park were spooky – witches' caverns with water bubbling through from miles back, from far away in the hills. And alongside the road ran a river, with ducks and geese and swirling waterweed.

"Witches' hair," said Tim, who was Ruthie's only friend. Together they gazed down into the water.

"This is a weird place," said Tim. "I get the feeling, all the time, that something not very nice is going to happen. Do you feel that?"

The others had hurtled across an ironwork bridge, towards the slides and swings. Underneath the swings was a carpet of soft, black squidgy stuff and Lisa and Bonk and Harry Chan kept falling off on purpose.

"Over here, Ruthie," yelled Lisa. "I'll give you a push."

Ruthie hated swings. She clung to the chains at either side until her palms and fingers hurt.

Grinning, Lisa pushed the swing harder and harder. It lifted Ruthie higher and higher until everything became a dizzy blur.

"Stop it! Stop it!" sobbed Ruthie. "I'm falling."

Miss O'Grady, who had been feeding two white geese on the river bank, shouted at Lisa, who let go her hold just as the swing catapulted Ruthie onto the ground. Gradually the swing lessened its impetus and became still. Lisa bent down towards Ruthie. "Scarebaby," she whispered, deep into Ruthie's ear.

Miss O'Grady sighed to see Lisa's dark head, vibrant with small tight plaits, against Ruthie's mousey-brown one. Ruthie was the only girl in the class to wear a hair-ribbon. An old-fashioned, pale pink hair-ribbon, holding Ruthie's thin lank hair back from her thin, pale face.

"I told you that something not very nice was going to happen," said Tim, squeezing Ruthie's arm.

But deep inside him a voice was saying, "Something is going to happen, but that's not it . . ."

Opposite the swings was a building with a big blue notice with the words HOLOGRAM GALLERY marked on it.

"That's wicked," shouted Bonk. "We went in one on holiday. Can we go there next, Miss?"

"May we please go to the chippy first?" asked Harry Chan, whose parents owned "The Blue Dolphin", at home in the shopping precinct.

"For goodness' sake, Harry, it isn't twelve o'clock yet," said Miss O'Grady.

"Mushy peas and battered saveloys," drooled Bonk.

"You cannot put batter on saveloys," said Harry Chan.

Not many of them could afford cod or haddock.

On the ground floor of the building was an amusement arcade, with loud music playing. Miss O'Grady hastily ushered her class up a flight of stairs at the side.

"What are holograms, Tim?" whispered Ruthie.

"They're just pictures, Ruthie. Three-dimensional pictures. I don't know how it's done, but when you look at them you feel you can reach out and touch them. But when you *do* try and touch them, then you find they're only flat pictures, after all."

Ruthie's eyes widened behind her pink-rimmed glasses.

"They're a sort of magic, but harmless magic," said Tim. "They're fun. You'll like them."

He followed Ruthie up the steps, the uneasy feeling inside him starting to grow.

The Hologram Gallery had rows of tall screens and on every screen glowed pictures, fluorescently bright. An oriental woman held out a bowl of tea, a girl hugged a baby lion, a winged monster reared up out of a magic forest. There was a picture called "The Witch's Kitchen" which showed an old woman in a black pointed hat reading something from a book of spells. A cauldron on a chain bubbled in one corner of the room and behind her were shelves of jars and books, and a book-end made from a grinning skull.

Class 4B soon lost its awe of the place and charged about, breathless with excitement.

"Look at the Cheshire cat," called Lisa, "Couldn't you just stroke it?" But her hand went through nothingness, and all she felt was the flat surface of the picture. It was the same with the champagne glass, held out enticingly on a tray, and with the puffer fish, green and prickly-looking, like a conker case.

"How do they do it, Miss?" asked Bonk, but

Miss O'Grady only shook her head, mystified.

"It's all done with mirrors and laser beams," said Harry Chan importantly. "The laser beams are split in two. My brother told me."

Tim was so busy going from picture to picture that he forgot about Ruthie. He did not see the way she pulled her hand quickly away from the Cheshire cat, the puffer fish, or how it lingered on the champagne glass.

For Ruthie, unlike the others, seemed in some strange way to be going into the extra dimension. She felt, ever so briefly, the warm fur of the Cheshire cat. The puffer fish pricked her like electricity. The champagne glass was cold to her touch.

Bonk had disappeared round a screen at the far end of the gallery.

"Come and look at this," he yelled. "This is the best of all. Really wicked!"

Lisa joined him and gave a shriek. The others gathered round.

"Skeletal Hands" the caption read and the bony, witch-like claws really seemed to stretch out of the picture, glinting in strange shades of green and turquoise, colours which merged and intertwined as you moved round them. There was a moment of silence, then, "How d'you do?" said Bonk, reaching out to shake the proffered claws.

"How d'you do?" screeched the others, laughing with relief as their hands passed through nothingness.

"Come on, Ruthie, shake claws," giggled Lisa, but Ruthie would not budge from the edge of the crowd.

"Scarebaby," taunted Lisa.

"Scarebaby," repeated Harry Chan.

Ruthie turned and ran.

"Come back, Ruthie," called Tim. But he could not find her.

Class 4B and Miss O'Grady clattered down the stairs, chattering excitedly. Tim followed, deciding that Ruthie must have run out into the street.

The gallery felt the hush, the silence. The overhead lights dimmed and a strange green light came rushing in, almost like water. Soon everything was bathed in it.

Ruthie, who had hidden behind one of the hologram screens, tiptoed through the empty hall and stood, trembling, before the picture of the Cheshire cat. The word "scarebaby" kept echoing through her.

91

Scarcely breathing, she reached up and touched the Cheshire cat. Her hand went through space and met the flat board of the picture. She touched it a second time, and a third. Relief flooded through her. She went to the puffer fish and touched it. Nothing but empty air. She touched the champagne glass and there was no cold sensation, no hard sensation.

"I imagined it," thought Ruthie. "I imagined it all!"

The skeletal hands were waiting, as claw-like, as witch-like as ever. Alone in the gallery, Ruthie felt a wave of stifling fear.

"I needn't touch them," she thought. "I've proved they're only pictures. I can leave now."

But in her head rang the taunts of Lisa and Harry Chan, "Scarebaby", "Scarebaby".

She held out her hand.

At the Promenade Fish Bar, Miss O'Grady was doing a head-count.

"One missing. There's one missing," she panicked.

"Is it Ruthie? Ruthie what's-her-name? Where is she?" said the deputy teacher.

"I think she might still be in the Hologram

place, Miss," said Tim, his pulse racing fast. "I'll go and look for her, shall I?"

"I'd better come as well," said Miss O'Grady. "The rest of you stay with Mrs Thomson and get on with your ordering. I don't understand this. It's not like Ruthie at all."

Tim, sick with foreboding, ran ahead and climbed the short flight of stairs into the hologram gallery. He moved dazedly through the weird green light, like a diver in deep water. As if in a nightmare, he bent to pick up the broken glasses, with pink frames, which lay underneath the picture of the skeletal hands. Straightening he saw, almost without shock, that the something which twined round the grisly, claw-like fingers was a ribbon of palest pink.

When he reached out to take the ribbon, his hand went through air and met the flat surface of the picture. But from somewhere behind the picture, as he peered intently through, came the sound of whimpering, becoming fainter and fainter – a whimpering so hopeless and terrified it struck a chill to the heart.

"Ruthie," whispered Tim. "Where are you, Ruthie?"

Coming out of his trance, he banged again and again at the picture on the wall. He moved round the gallery, searching each picture intently, until he reached "The Witch's Kitchen".

The old crone, who before had been looking down at a book of spells on the table, was now staring directly at him. And the eyes, he saw with shock, were the pale blue, terrified eyes of Ruthie.

He tore downstairs, yelling for Miss O'Grady.

"Steady, lad," said the man at the cash desk. "She's gone back along the street with the coach driver. They've found your friend. She's sitting in the coach."

While the coach driver was finding Miss O'Grady, Lisa had gone back to the coach park. She had discovered, when about to pay for her fish and chips, that she must have left her purse in the coach.

"What are you doing here, Ruthie?" asked Lisa, climbing on board. "Everybody's looking for you."

Staring straight ahead, Ruthie did not reply.

"Are you all right?" asked Lisa. "Are you feeling sick or something?"

She moved towards the figure slumped in the back seat of the coach, leant towards her, and drew in her breath with shock. For the face that looked up at her was Ruthie's face but the eyes, green and bright with animal cunning, were not.

Lisa felt her wrist being seized in a vice-like grip and Ruthie's silver and mother-of-pearl ring being wrenched from her little finger.

"Stop it!" cried Lisa "Stop it, Ruthie – you're hurting me!"

"Scarebaby," cackled Ruthie, in a voice unlike her own.

Then Lisa screamed so loudly it brought Tim and Miss O'Grady and the driver racing towards the coach.

For the hand that grasped Lisa was a witch-like claw, with fingers as bony as a skeleton's. And, try as they might, they could not loosen its hold on her.

Fitted Carpets

Mum goes out to work and our flat is always a bit of a clutter, but between us we manage to keep it clean and it's always cheerful and bright. Mum's let me paint the walls – really paint them, with pictures, I mean – and she makes cushions and beanbags and we scatter them all over. We've lots of plants, too, for the oxygen – busy lizzies and prayer-plants and even a cheese-plant that was left out for the dustmen when an office on the main road went bust – but nothing, absolutely nothing, like the plant I'm going to tell you about.

* * *

I've always wanted a dog, but Mum said no – not in a flat in the middle of North London. It's bad enough, she says, having other people's dogs roaming round in packs because their owners can't be bothered to look after them. It's a bit like stepping out into the jungle, with animals snapping and snarling at each other's legs – and once there was a big green parrot which flapped its wings and made squawking noises. The parrot didn't just squawk, either. It made sounds like car brakes squealing (straight from Miami Vice) and when workmen went past the window it wolf-whistled. Mrs Benson was always complaining about the parrot noises.

We weren't going to have an animal at all, but then this lop-eared moggy with one eye sort of adopted us. We're three floors up, but Mum worked out that it could climb up a drainpipe and along a window ledge, so we made a cat-flap for it. We call it Horace. I don't know why. It's a funny cat and growls sometimes, just like a dog.

My friend Barry wanted a cat, or gerbils, or a stick insect – anything. But Mrs Benson, Barry's mum, wouldn't hear of it. Mrs Benson was very houseproud. When you went into her front room you had to take your shoes off, so an animal with muddy paws was out of the question. Mrs Benson was always moaning about our block of flats – the damp walls, the state of the corridors. She had her eye on a choice block just down the road – all white net curtains and little laid-out gardens like pocket handkerchiefs, which the council men came and tidied up every month. There was one window, though, that didn't have net curtains and that was where the parrot lived.

The parrot was large and green, with a fiery red head which it cocked to one side when it was studying a new and interesting noise. Between our block and the parrot's block was a big gate that needed oil on its hinges. The Caley twins took to swinging on this gate, and it was an hour before anybody stopped them. An hour was all the parrot needed, as it stood in the open window, head turning this way and that. After three hours of creaking-gate noises, parrot-version, Mrs Benson knocked on the door of our flat, flushed and furious in her headscarf and spotless pinny.

"I'm going to report her to the council," she said. "Keeping pets shouldn't be allowed. It's a waste of a beautiful flat. She doesn't appreciate it, does she? Look at the outside of it – you can just imagine the inside. When I think what I could do with a flat like that! Central heating, fitted carpets. But it's no use bothering in *this* place, is it?"

The parrot belonged to an old lady, and for some time Mrs Benson had had her eye on the old lady's flat. It was true she made rather a mess of the garden, putting out boxes and piles of newspaper and cracked pots. The council men who came to do the garden cleared away the mess, but it always reappeared a few days afterwards. Someone had thrown a stone at the window once, and the old lady had mended the crack with what looked like sticking plaster. Barry said she was a witch, but that was only what his mother had told him. When we went to knock on her door at Hallowe'en, he ran off and hid.

My friend Jackie and I were Spirits of the Dead and Ahmed, her younger brother, had dressed himself as Mighty Mouse. After peering at us from her doorway for a moment or two, the old lady seemed quite glad to see us. She shuffled her way to the kitchen for a box of biscuits and so we were able to get a good look at the hall. There was a spotted skin rug on the floor with the animal's head on it – staring eyes, big teeth, the lot. Ahmed asked if he could stroke it. Then she asked if we would like to see her parrot.

The parrot looked at us suspiciously and made chuntering noises, lifting one claw off the windowsill and then the other. Some of its tailfeathers were missing. The old lady told us that it was forty years old – older than Mum – imagine it! She said her husband had been a doctor in South America and they had brought the parrot back to England with them. They had lived in a clearing in a rain forest, in a hut with a low thatched roof, and kept pigs and chickens, but the natives of the forest were hunters and would not eat tame animals. She said there were man-eating jaguars in the forest, and monkeys and tree-frogs and anacondas – great green snakes that crushed their prey to death before swallowing them.

She had holes in the elbows of her cardigan, but talked in a posh sort of voice and her surname had two parts to it, but I can't remember what they were. The room was untidy and shabby, but there were interesting things everywhere – brightly-coloured woven mats on the walls and floors, and animals carved out of wood. A tall plant with dark green leaves stood in a heavy clay pot. The pot had a strange-looking bird's head with a big golden eye painted on it. The old lady said it was a forest spirit. She said that when the people who lived in the forest killed a bird or animal, its spirit took revenge on them. Perhaps Mrs Benson was right and she was batty, after all.

Later that night Barry joined up with the Caley twins and they went round playing tricks on people. I don't know how he managed to pick up Horace, because Horace will only let me and Mum touch him but, anyway, somehow he managed to get Horace into the old lady's garden. Barry told me afterwards that Horace hadn't even touched the bird, just stood in the garden and looked up at it, but the bird had no sooner fixed its beady eye on Horace than it rose in a flurry of feathers, squawked and fell lifeless on the windowsill. Perhaps it had a heart attack – it was forty years old, which seems a good lifespan for a bird. Anyway, I couldn't really blame Horace and Barry was very sorry about it.

But after the death of the parrot, the old lady became stranger and stranger. She closed up the window and put a striped blanket across it and, now there was no bird to buy food for, she never seemed to go out at all, except to tip rubbish in the garden. Mrs Benson, who bought Barry a bike even though it wasn't his birthday, started making friends with the other people in the old lady's block. You could see them pointing at the rubbish and shaking their heads over their own neat pots of geraniums. And Barry told me his mum was writing letters to the council.

They took the old lady away, one fine spring morning, to a nursing home called West Winds, known to us kids on the estate as the Funny Farm. Everything in the flat was cleared out and auctioned off, except for the plant in the living room. Perhaps the pot was too heavy to move, or perhaps they just forgot it. Mum gave it some water when she was helping Mrs Benson measure for carpets and curtains. Mum asked Mrs Benson if she would like her to take the plant away and was surprised to hear Mrs Benson say she would measure round it. Mrs Benson had never shown any liking for plants before, and the only flowers she put in her vases were plastic ones. Mum hadn't liked the way Mrs Benson had gone on about the old lady and then moved into her flat, but she owed her some favours. They swept and scrubbed and scoured everything, and then the van arrived with the carpets. They were a pale grey colour, with big, squashy pink roses.

The next week Mrs Benson asked Mum and

me round for tea, as a thank you for the help
Mum had given her. We had to take our shoes
off, of course, so as not to dirty the fitted
carpets. Everything was neat and tidy and spotless, and instead of a parrot messing up the
windowsill there was a row of glazed pottery
ducks on the wall. Only the plant looked out of
place. It stood in its big clay pot with the
glowering golden eye, right in the middle of a
pattern of squashy roses. I thought of what the
old lady had said about forest spirits and the
revenge they took. And it made me shiver a bit.

"That plant's getting bigger every day," said
Mrs Benson. "I wonder what sort of a plant it
is? I've never seen one like it in Marks and
Spencer."

Mum saw, on looking closely, that one of the
flowers had come out. It was a sort of bell
shape, like the white flowers that twine across
the tops of the garages and hang down drain-
pipes. But this flower was pink – not the bright
pink of the roses on Mrs Benson's carpet but a
dull, fleshy pink. There were rows of spiky
hairs on every petal and the smell that came
from it was horrible, like decaying meat. It
nearly put me off my tea.

After tea, when we were watching television,
Mrs Benson gave a little cry of fright. She

jumped out of her armchair.

"Did you see that?" she gasped. "Something just ran across the carpet."

I had seen some movement from the corner of my eye. It was a scurrying sort of movement, as if a spider, or even a small animal, had crossed the room. Mr Benson rolled up a newspaper and peered behind the chair, but he could not find anything.

Then suddenly the room seemed to be buzzing with flies – big, black, noisy flies – worrying their shadows on the wall, swinging on the lampshade, settling in the jam. Mrs Benson screamed again. Mr Benson wielded his newspaper. I was standing by the plant when a black, glittering fly settled on it. The fly, attracted by the strong smell of meat, crawled further and further down the middle of the flower. Suddenly the hairs on the petals snapped shut like a metal trap. I could almost hear the click. Barry was looking over my shoulder, his eyes nearly popping out of his head.

"It caught it," he whispered. "It caught the fly. It's going to *eat* it."

It was a week later when I next went to call on Barry. He looked a bit odd when I knocked on the door.

"Wait here," he said. "I'll be out in a minute."

The hall looked dusty and dirty and the milk bottles on the step had not been washed out properly. I asked him if his mum was ill. He shook his head.

It was the first really hot day of the year and we sat on the roof of the garages to do our homework. The roofs were made of corrugated iron and were quite hot to sit on. Round the garages was a patch of land covered with weeds where Horace liked to stalk around, pretending to be a tiger. Insects were buzzing everywhere and even some butterflies hovered above the yellow gorsey flowers and thistles. I sat up suddenly.

"What's your mum doing down there?" I asked. "With that butterfly net?"

Barry shrugged and looked embarrassed. Then he said:

"She's catching insects."

"Catching insects? What for?"

"For that plant. It's all she ever does these days. Looks after it, waters it, feeds it. Dad and me have to get our own food. She even feeds it spiders. She never used to dare touch a spider."

"Has the plant grown even bigger?" I asked.

"You'd better come and look," said Barry.

105

The stench inside the room was even more horrible. I felt myself retching. The plant had grown to twice its former size and flesh-coloured flowers sprouted all over it. The room had a neglected look. Patches of damp were showing on the walls. Even the new carpet looked damp in places and the atmosphere was airless, humid. For a moment I thought I heard a chirping – a chirping of birds, or insects – the sort of noise you get in Tarzan films.

"Did you hear that?" I asked.

"What?" asked Barry. He looked very sorry for himself.

Two days later we heard the wail of a police siren. Barry banged on our door sobbing, his face and neck covered in sweat.

"Come quick," he yelled. "You've got to help us. The plant's got Mum."

The stench of decaying meat had spread throughout the flat now. The policemen, swearing, hacked their way through a room choked with moist, dense, tropical vegetation. Their feet sank into what was no longer a carpet of patterned roses, but slimy green moss. The plant had spread itself all over the living room – across the walls, along pictures – and coiled, snakelike, round and round the stem of Mrs

Benson's reading lamp. Small bright birds and chattering monkeys balanced on its tendrils. The room was a clamour of bird noise, rustling insects, the mating call of frogs. And round the room, swooping and screeching, flew a great green parrot with a head the colour of blood.

Mrs Benson stood in the midst of it all, her wrist in the vice-like grip of hairy, fleshy petals. The fingers of one hand held a wriggling spider, the fingers of the other had disappeared down the flower's hungry throat. Dazed, unseeing, she did not react to the sight of us, or when the policeman moved towards her, but every now and then she would utter a short, sharp scream.

Barry spent that night on a beanbag on the floor of our front room. He said she was screaming like that all the way to West Winds.

The Witch at the Window

If Lucinda had not been born with a silver spoon in her mouth, it must at least have been a silver-plated one. And probably with a pattern of pink enamelled roses as well. For Lucinda was a very "pink roses" little girl. She had pink roses on her party dress and pink roses on her bedroom wallpaper. The paintwork of her bedroom, too, was sugary pink.

"Sugar and spice and all things nice," cooed her grandmother fondly. "That's what little girls are made of."

Lucinda did not have to share her grandmother with any brother or sister, or any cousins either. Because she was the only child in the family, all her aunts and uncles made a great fuss of her and gave her lovely presents at birthday and Christmas times – white fluffy toys and pretty rings and necklaces. All, that is, except Aunt Morag. Aunt Morag loomed like the unwanted fairy godmother at all family gatherings. While the rest of the adults sipped sweet sherry and talked about the state of the weather and the Stock Exchange, Aunt Morag sat silent and glowering in a haze of cigarette smoke. Lucinda's mother would tut and open doors and windows, but she never dared to ask Aunt Morag to smoke outside.

Once, Lucinda and her parents had actually been to stay with Aunt Morag at her ivy-strangled cottage in the country. It had been a terrible experience. Lucinda had had to wash in cold water and suffer at night in a narrow, lumpy bed, staring in terror at a cobweb on the ceiling, expecting that at any moment a hairy black spider would descend from it and land on her face. Aunt Morag had made her get up at seven to feed squawking, vicious hens and a big fat pig which gave out disgusting grunting noises and kept pressing its filthy body against Lucinda. Aunt Morag told her a story about a neighbouring farmer who had fallen asleep in his pig-pen and how his favourite sow had started to eat his foot! It was with indescribable relief that Lucinda returned home to her own comfortable sunny room, and her big soft quilt with flowers and pierrots on it.

As her eighth birthday approached, Lucinda did wonder once or twice what her present from Aunt Morag would be. Last year's present, a chemistry set, still lay untouched in its box. Lucinda had been born at the loveliest time of the year, of course – the month of May – and as her birthday fell this time on a Saturday, her mother prepared her a special birthday breakfast and arranged all the colourful and beribboned packages from doting aunts and uncles carefully round it.

It was obvious, thought Lucinda, which present was from Aunt Morag. Amidst the candy stripes and little shining stars and frilled rosettes sat a book-shaped object, hastily wrapped in brown paper and tied, Lucinda noted disdainfully, with the rough green string Aunt Morag used for her broad beans and dahlias. Lucinda decided to open the ugly brown parcel last – the other gifts looked so much more attractive. But even as she oohed and aahed at the silver bracelet, the china kitten, the box of strawberry creams, Lucinda was wondering, at the back of her mind, just what sort of a book her least favourite aunt had given her.

When she finally tore open the brown paper and stared at the book, it was with a sense of deep disappointment. She had, at least, expected something unusual. But all Aunt Morag had sent was a copy of "Hansel and Gretel". Hansel and Gretel indeed! What a babyish story! Surely Aunt Morag realized she was eight years old now?

Lucinda had first heard "Hansel and Gretel" when she was five and had not liked it at all. She had not been able to understand how the mother and father in the story could deliberately lose their children in the forest, no matter how poor they might be. The deep forest had frightened her and when she came to the part of the story where Hansel and Gretel find the gingerbread house, and the ugly old woman who turns out to be a witch – a witch who plans to roast the children in her oven and eat them! – she could listen no more. Lucinda's mother, alarmed at her sobs, hastily removed "Hansel and Gretel" and replaced it with a book called "Flower Fairies of the Dell". And Lucinda had thought no more about Hansel and Gretel until her eighth birthday when, staring down at her present, she decided that Aunt Morag must surely have sent it out of spite.

To add insult to injury, there were not even words in the book. It was just a series of pictures – of the pop-up variety, which seemed to spring to life whenever one turned a page. The first page showed the woodcutter's cottage at the edge of the forest. The trees were very realistic-looking. As the page opened they trembled, as if a breeze was passing through them. The second page showed Hansel and Gretel in the deep, dark forest. Lucinda shivered a little when she saw that. But on the third page the children were back home again. The fourth page pictured an even deeper part of the forest and the gingerbread house, with its roof of marzipan and icing and windows of frosted sugar. On the fifth page one of the windows sprang open to reveal a hideous witch. Lucinda screamed and closed the book quickly. She expected her mother to come running into the room to ask what the matter was, but her mother was having words outside with the milkman, and didn't hear her. Lucinda opened the book at the fifth page a second time, very slowly, peeped at the horrible grey-faced crone, with hair like matted rope, and shut the book again.

That night, long after her light had been put out, and her parents were downstairs talking,

Lucinda opened the book and shone her torch into the witch's face.

"You don't frighten me," she whispered, "you don't frighten me at all!"

In the torchlight the witch's eyes shone green as glass. There was even a spot of saliva on her chin. Lucinda closed the book quickly, hurrying barefoot from the room. Her toes sank into the thick pile of the landing carpet. On the landing was a cupboard which her mother used for storing towels and linen. Lucinda pushed the book into the cupboard and closed the door firmly. Then she tiptoed back to bed, still trembling a little.

Later that night she dreamed that she was wandering about inside the book. She was lost in the forest and hungry. The trees overhead were gaunt and dark, rustling like paper. The knots of the trunks had faces on them. The floor of the forest was slippery, like the surface of a page.

"Face number five," a voice kept whispering. "Face number five."

Lucinda moved, with difficulty, to the fifth tree and pressed the knot on its bark. The wooden face seemed familiar. Then, somehow, she had passed through the tree and there in front of her was the gingerbread house, glowing

golden in the darkness of the forest. She saw
that the pillars of the house were made of
twisted barley-sugar and her mouth watered.
She stretched out her hand to break off a piece,
but suddenly there was Aunt Morag, actually
smiling at her from the window of the gingerbread house. Aunt Morag beckoned, but as
Lucinda moved towards her the smile became a
hideous scowl and her teeth rotted black as
liquorice.

"It's the witch!" screamed Lucinda.

Aunt Morag set up a repulsive cackling. She
reached out a claw-like hand and shook
Lucinda, who awoke to find herself in bed and
being shaken by her mother, with her own
sweet smile and teeth as white as mint
imperials.

"You've been dreaming," whispered Lucinda's mother. "Wake up now, gently does it.
Why are you staring at me like that, darling? Is
something wrong?"

Lucinda shook her head, but even as she
cuddled up to her mother, she was half afraid
of her turning into a witch as well. When
morning came she fetched the book from the
linen cupboard and, with half-closed eyes, cut
out the witch from the window, scrunching her
up into a tight little ball and dropping her into

the waste paper basket.

After that, Lucinda lost interest in the present from Aunt Morag. It lay, unopened, at the back of her toy-shelf, throughout the months of June and July. In August came the school holidays and Lucinda, when deciding what to pack for the seaside, glanced at it again. But she felt no desire to open the book. The witch had gone, so there seemed no point in it.

They took Grandma with them to the hotel at the seaside, but Lucinda had a room to herself. The room was painted blue, with pretty sea-shell-patterned walls. There was a poodle made of seashells on the bedside table, and a tiny balcony with a view of the sea.

The weather was sunny, with a pleasant salty breeze. Lucinda paddled in the sea, and when the water lapped against her knees she felt very daring. Her mother and father read books under beach umbrellas and Grandma snoozed. One day a group of rather scruffy-looking boys started aiming pebbles into a nearby rockpool and the water splashed over Grandma's lap. Lucinda's father stood up angrily and the boys ran off, shouting with laughter.

"Rats and snails and puppy-dogs' tails," muttered Grandma, mopping herself with a starched handkerchief. "That's what little *boys* are made of".

Towards the end of the first week of the holiday, Grandma decided to have her afternoon nap at the hotel while Lucinda and her mother and father went for a special trip in a steam train. They chugged through the gently undulating countryside. Cows and trees and farmers on red tractors sailed sedately past the windows. There were old-fashioned, brown-coloured prints above the seats of the train.

"Tickets, please," said a man in a spankingly smart uniform. He smiled at Lucinda. "Next stop Sandhaven."

"I'm not so sure that I *would* want steam trains back again," said Lucinda's mother, as she negotiated the steep drop onto the platform. "It does seem to create rather a lot of mess. Look at those smudges on your white dress, darling."

The little station had boxes of brightly-coloured geraniums and a brown and gold metal sign which read WELCOME TO SAND-HAVEN.

"It's like stepping back in time," said Lucinda's father. "It's a shame Grandma didn't come."

116

The village seemed to be in league with the railway company. The little tea-shops offering scones and jam, the antique shops with their gleaming brasses, all had an olde-worlde look to them.

"I wonder if property is very expensive?" whispered Lucinda's mother. "It would be rather nice to live here, wouldn't it, John?"

Then, as they turned a corner into a side-street, she cried out, "Oh, look at that sweet-shop. Isn't it lovely?"

Lucinda stared. The shop was painted up like a golden gingerbread house. The pillars on either side of the door were twisted like barley-sugar and the roof shone like an iced cake. Behind frosted windows, with round humbugs set into them, stood rows of jars of multi-coloured sweets.

"We must buy something," laughed Lucinda's mother. "It takes me back to my child-hood. It's a Hansel and Gretel house."

Lucinda followed her mother and father into the shop slowly, nervously. It was true there had been no hideous face at the window, but what might be lurking in the dark corners of the quaint little shop, behind the sherbet dips, the jars of jelly beans?

"I'll be with you in a moment," called out a

pleasant, sing-song voice, and out of the shadows came a plump, rosy-faced, smiling little old woman with candid blue eyes and hair scraped back into a neat bun.

Lucinda breathed a huge sigh of relief and, as her parents were enjoying themselves so much, she began to enjoy herself, too. She chose half a pound of striped humbugs, three dear little white sugar mice with pink noses and, yes, as her fears settled themselves for ever, two long, elaborate coils of blackest liquorice. The little old lady chatted amiably about this and that as she weighed out the sweets for them, and when they left she waved goodbye from between the sugar portals, her smile as warm as fudge straight from the oven.

Lucinda's mother had bought a bag of big, squashy marshmallows, and on the train going back she offered them round.

"So soon after that enormous cream tea," she sighed. "I am making a pig of myself. Would you like one, Lucinda dear?"

Lucinda shook her head. She felt too full for marshmallows. I might, she thought, manage a minty humbug, though.

Feeling stickily into the paper bag, trying to dislodge one humbug from another, she thought she felt something move. The humbugs seemed to have a different feel to them – colder, more fragile, somehow. And the stickiness underneath them – wasn't that more of a slime? Peering into the bag, she saw with amazement that it was full of snails – moving snails with tiny horns and black and yellow striped shells on their backs.

Suddenly the three sugar mice leapt from her pocket. They skittled across the floor of the compartment, baring their teeth like angry rats, growing larger, becoming furry.

The coils of liquorice slithered, snake-like, to join them – lurching, wriggling, *wagging* almost, just like –

A whistle blew, high and shrill, the screeching of a banshee. Lucinda froze. She could hear it now – the witch's laughter. She could see the grey, gnarled grinning face at the window of the train. The laughter went on and on, high-pitched and hysterical. The whistle blew like a chorus of banshees, the face turned into the face of Aunt Morag, and the train plunged headlong into a long, dark, never-ending tunnel.

A Pocket of Posies

He would never, thought Roland, get used to the silence of living in the country. It made the smallest sound more disturbing – the tick of a beetle in the wainscot, the rustling of leaves in the linden trees which sheltered the churchyard next to the cottage.

It was a stone cottage Mum had bought, high in the Peak District, the end cottage of a row. "Plague Cottages" they were called, in memory of a terrible epidemic back in the seventeenth century which had wiped out most of the village. So many people died that the churchyard could not hold them. They had been buried out in the fields and hills – and sometimes even

120

under the floors of houses.

Downstairs a door opened and music wafted up. Dylan again. Mum had been playing all her old Dylan records lately.

> "My love she laughs like the flowers –
> Valentines cannot buy her."

How could anyone laugh like flowers? It did not mean anything. Or perhaps it did. Mum's face had opened up a lot since she met Quinn. Roland had not liked Quinn at first. He had not trusted him. He was so much younger than Mum – only ten years older than Roland.

They had met Quinn up in the hills when they had been looking for flowers for Mum to photograph. They had come across the peculiar "bender", a shelter made from tarpaulin and the branches of trees, where Quinn lived. Quinn had tied bells and bits of coloured glass to the branches. He said he saw rainbows every morning – a real throwback hippy, thought Roland scornfully.

The only good thing about Quinn was that he would never stay in the village for long. He felt that there were bad vibrations from all the people who had died there. He had gone all funny when Mum had shown him Mary

Teylor's grave and the pocket of posies.

The grave was in the cellar. Mum and Roland had found it when they were clearing out the cellar to make a dark room for Mum. It was cold down there, clammy and cold. They had been reading the headstone, set in the icy stone floor, when Sydney the cat had pounced on a mouse. Mum had forced Sydney's mouth open and the mouse had run behind a shelf of old glass bottles. And stuffed down behind the shelf, covered in bits of broken plaster, they had found the leather pouch.

Mum had been really excited. She said it was a "pocket of posies" – something people in the old days had carried round with them to try to ward off the plague. But when they had opened up the pouch, easing apart the cords which fastened the neck of it, there had been an acrid, bitter smell.

"My love she laughs like the flowers –
    Valentines cannot buy her."

Mary Teylor had laughed like those flowers. Bitter laughter, full of hatred, thought Roland, and shivered. Moonlight, pale as moths' wings, fluttered through the half-open window and disappeared into the dark corners of the room.

Mary Teylor had gone from the house. She could not harm him now.

They had met Quinn again when in the Dell, picking flowers for the well-dressings. The weather had been airless and hot – unusual for that part of the country. They had scrambled up the steep slopes of the Dell searching for footholes, clutching at great clumps of vegetation, the sun beating down hard on the backs of their necks, the pigsty smell of meadowsweet all around them. Once at the top, the land dipped suddenly and there was the great hole in the limestone rock where, in plague days, the preacher had prayed out of doors to his congregation – or what was left of it.

Mum had been scraping lichen from the rocks for some time before they noticed Quinn. He was sitting on one of the stones which formed a natural sort of pew, staring at the land and sky in front of him. They had sat and talked with him a little and a browney-green insect had hopped onto Roland's knee.

Quinn said it was a cricket, and that it was a good thing the cricket was green because a white cricket meant that plague would visit the house. He said that local people would never take may blossom into their homes, because that meant the plague would come too. Mum said it was all nonsense, because the plague was driven out years ago. But Quinn said that a hundred years after the plague had left the village, some men working on the hillside had dug up pieces of linen cloth and all three died within a week from a mysterious fever.

Then they walked down to the village hall, where people were busy making floral pictures to dress the wells – to-ing and fro-ing with sheaves of grasses and buckets of petals. It was an annual event, the dressing and blessing of the wells, and the whole village took part. Mrs Heald, the Post Office lady, had almost finished her picture. Roland watched as she pressed red rose and blue hydrangea petals into soft, damp soil to complete a counterpane. Then she stepped back from the wooden frame to show him the picture in full.

She had chosen, like so many others, to depict a scene from the seventeenth century. But the woman in the picture wore not Puritan clothes, but a long white flowing dress, and she was bending over a man as he lay in bed. Mrs Heald said the idea for the picture came from an old village story, but before Roland could ask her about it Mum came over to say that

Quinn was going home with them to collect some water.

He stayed for a meal, of course, and it was then that Mum showed him the leather pouch.

Quinn went peculiar when he saw it. He said she must burn it. But Mum could be stubborn when she wanted to. She said that the next time she went to London she would take it to the British Museum. Quinn went back to his bender after that, and Roland begged Mum to let him hang the pouch in his bedroom. He wanted to show her that he was not afraid of it, even if Quinn was.

It was that night that he first felt the presence in his bedroom. He had difficulty in sleeping because of the heat. The hands on his clock showed a quarter to three. There seemed to be a shadow in the room. Although the room was hot and airless, the leather pouch, hanging from a picture hook in the wall, started swinging to and fro, gently at first. There was a bitter smell about the place – bitter herbs, bitter flowers – and the shadow was moving towards him. As Roland lay rigid with terror, a faint whispering began. It was speaking his name, over and over again, and muttering unintelligible words.

He thought he heard whatever it was say,
  "Roland – hast thou forgotten me?"

Then the shadow moved away from him towards the open window, where it melted into the moonlight.

There was a faint crying sound outside his bedroom door. Roland leapt out of bed and flung the door open. Sydney the cat stood there, her back arched and her fur ridged with fear.

The thought, the next day, that the experience had been a vivid dream, stopped him from telling Mum about it. But he knew he would have to go down to the cellar and read the headstone again. He kept putting it off, until Mum asked him to go down for a bottle of wine. She said that Quinn might be calling for a meal again.

Hatred of Quinn forced him down the cellar steps and he groped about for the bottle, his hands clutching at cobwebs gritty with flies. Quinn had been afraid to look at the headstone so he, Roland, would not be afraid. He read the ancient inscription over and over:

Here li'th ye body of Mary Teylor bu
ried by this stone. Who Dyed on Aug. ye
25 Day 1666
Lyk a shadow

Mary Teylor had lived in the house, had died of the plague there. So much was clear. But if she had been the woman in his dream, who had she been talking to? Him, of course. She had been talking to him.

"Roland . . . hast thou forgotten me?"

How could I have forgotten her, he thought, when I did not even know her? She had lived in the seventeenth century – more than three hundred years ago.

Mum called to him to hurry up. She was going to see a woman at the top end of the village, to look at some fancy-dress costumes. It would soon be Wakes Day, when the people in the village dressed up and rode around on floats. Mum said it would be a chance for him to get to know some of the young people in the village, before school started in the autumn.

They climbed and climbed, leaving behind the old stone cottages, painted black and white, with hanging baskets of flowers. The two houses on the top edge of the village were large and modern-looking, perched over a huge sweep of trees and moorland. Roland did not fancy trying on costumes, so he climbed over a stile into a steep field, where cows were grazing.

As he walked into the field the cows edged away from him, revealing a small walled enclosure with a stone sarcophagus inside it. A step led into the enclosure. Roland hesitated. He wondered if something bad would happen if he stepped through. A blue butterfly settled on a thistle flower just inside the wall. Roland leaned over to read from the stone the names of a father, mother, son and two daughters – Martha and Aleis – who had died of the plague in 1666. The surname of the family was Teylor.

Roland sat down by the wall, in the sunshine, his heart beating fast. Had Mary Teylor been another daughter? But why was she not buried up there on the hillside? Why was her body in the cellar at home? In those days, young women left home only to marry, and Mary Teylor had never married, even if she had intended to.

"Roland . . . Hast thou forgotten me?"

After what seemed like an age, Mum emerged with two large packages. She put them on top of the stile and climbed over to join Roland. He showed her the sarcophagus, but he did not say anything about the name of the family and she did not seem to make the connection.

Together they walked further down the field to where Mum said there was something called a "vinegar stone". A notice read that in the time of the plague an indentation in the rock was filled with vinegar, supposedly to purify the money that the family on the hillside had put there, and in return people from the village left food for them.

Mum said the costumes were from a play the villagers had put on a few years before. She said the woman in the house had told her that the plague had started up there on the hillside, in a remote farmhouse. She said that when the plague had spread, another vinegar stone had been used on the other side of the village.

From that part of the field, despite the distance, they could see down into the village quite clearly. They could see the stocks, and the village green with the Dell behind it. It was warm on the hillside, but then a chill wind blew.

When they had arrived back home, Quinn had been sitting on the doorstep. He stayed for dinner and Mum took out the costume she had borrowed for Roland. It was a costume from Puritan times – black coat and knee breeches and a big black hat. Roland reluctantly tried on the knee breeches. They fitted quite well, but the coat had some buttons missing. Mum found her button-box and dropped it, and buttons rolled about everywhere. Quinn scrabbled on the floor for buttons and then put on the tall black hat. Mum said it suited him, especially with the beard, and that she would take some photographs. Roland said he was not going to wear the silly costume and stamped upstairs.

Later, in his dreams, the woman visited him again. Her face was close to his. She had eyes the colour of violets and thick black eyelashes. This time he heard what she was saying quite clearly.

"I will thee wed, Roland," and "Hast thou forgotten me?"

She held up her hand and petals showered his sleeping head and shoulders. Rose and hydrangea, like velvety summer rain. He tossed this way and that in the softness and the suffocating fragrance. When he awoke there were no petals, just an acrid smell in the room.

The next day, Wakes Day, was the anniversary of Mary Teylor's death.

Wakes Day dawned clear and bright, the sky a washed-out blue. People from the row of cottages were putting chairs and tables out into their front gardens and, in the distance somewhere, a brass band was playing.

Mum came into Roland's bedroom to show

130

him her outfit. She was dressed as a woman from Puritan times – the time of the plague – in a plain black dress with white starched collar and folded white head-dress. Roland grumbled about the heavy costumes, saying that the weather would be too hot for them.

Quinn arrived at about mid-morning. He had not put on fancy dress but then, thought Roland, he did not need to. Quinn was resplendent in an embroidered silk waistcoat and baggy trousers. His russet-coloured hair was partly braided, and dangling from one ear was a brightly-painted wooden parrot. He held a can of beer in each hand.

The floats started to wobble their way along the main street – "Snow White and the Seven Dwarfs", an Egyptian float called "Full of Eastern Promise" and a seventeenth-century tableau – "The Vinegar Stone" – which showed a woman taking food from beside a large stone and dropping coins into an indentation in the stone, filled with vinegar.

Roland wandered along the main street, hot inside his costume but glad of the big, black hat. A man with knobbly knees, dressed as a charwoman, approached him, rattling a tin. He turned into the church. It was full of trippers buying postcards and books, and children running up and down the aisles, licking ice-creams.

Roland sank into a pew on the south aisle, as far away from other people as possible. He rested his head on his hands for a few minutes and pretended to pray. His eyes became accustomed to the gloom and took in a wall-bracket, which held a wooden, foreign-looking statue of the Virgin and Child. Beneath the bracket was an open register, in a glass frame. Moving closer, he saw that the top page was covered in spidery black writing spelling out the names of people who had died in the plague. The list went on, endlessly. A child ran across to him, stood on tiptoe and rubbed sticky fingers across the glass.

Roland went out into the churchyard, past the ancient Celtic cross, and gazed up at the inscription on the stone corbels of the sundial.

"UT UMBRA SIC VITA"

"Like a shadow, so passes life"

He shivered and walked towards the village green, where people were dancing to a piped band. Mum and Quinn were dancing and Quinn was making an exhibition of himself. Mum was laughing and gazing at Quinn as if only the two of them existed.

The feeling that came over Roland was so violent that he had to sit down on the old wooden stocks at the edge of the Green. He closed his eyes tight shut and squeezed his fists into them – and when he opened them, just for a second or two, the scene had changed.

The woman in the old-fashioned frock was not Mum any more and the man was not Quinn. The music was different, too. It came from a corner of the green where a man played a pipe to a dancing bear. Then things were back to normal again, and Mum was still dancing with Quinn.

At last Mum spotted Roland and, leaving Quinn behind, they walked together back to the main street, by the horse trough, where a sheep-roast was in progress. Mum said that Quinn disapproved of the sheep-roast, being a vegetarian, but Roland was hardly listening. He was staring at the flowing white dress of the woman ahead of them in the queue. He had seen the dress before, but in the darkness of his room he had not recognized what it was. A wedding dress.

Some youths in the crowd were getting boisterous. They jostled Roland, pushing him against the woman in front. She turned towards him in her white gown, and underneath the head-dress were empty eye sockets and two rows of grinning teeth.

Roland gave a cry. He lost his footing and

fell against the stone trough and all was darkness. When he came to he was in the kitchen at home, and Mum and Quinn and the woman were bending over him.

The woman in the white dress showed him the rubber skeleton mask she had been wearing under her veil. Her name was Jane Heald, the daughter of the Post Office lady, and she had borrowed her dress from the same place as Mum. She said that she knew it would fit, because she had worn it in the village play. She had taken the part of Mary Teylor, a young and beautiful girl from the farm on the hillside. Mary had been betrothed to a young man from the village, and the young man had lived, all those years ago, in the cottage that Roland's Mum had bought.

As Jane Heald talked on, Roland began to feel drowsy. Mum wanted to call a doctor, but he insisted he would be all right. Mum said she would make him a cup of tea, and put some brandy in it.

There was a fireplace in the kitchen, although with it being a hot day in August no fire was lit. Sydney the cat seemed to be stalking something in the hearth. Roland, alone at last, craned his neck but could see nothing, not even a spider or a half-stunned fly.

He lay back in the chair, racking his brains about something he had seen on his way from the church to the village green. Then he remembered. Mrs Heald's well-dressing picture had been vandalized. Someone had made a great hole in the counterpane of red rose and blue hydrangea petals. Roland thought of the petals which he had felt showering over him the night before. He remembered the picture, of the woman in the long white dress bending over the man as he lay in bed. And, at the bottom of the picture, the message picked out in black sunflower seeds against a white rose background: "The Kiss of Death".

After they had all drunk some tea, Roland dozed off to sleep in the kitchen and Mum and Quinn tiptoed quietly into the front room. How long he slept he could not tell, but when he awoke the room was darker. He found himself gazing at a round, white object which lay on the kitchen hearth-rug. It was a large mother-of-pearl button, dropped there when Mum had upset her button-box the evening before. As Roland continued to look, the button became bigger, grew legs, and took on the shape of a white cricket.

There was a sudden movement from Sydney the cat and the cricket disappeared. Had it gone up the chimney, wondered Roland? He rose stiffly from the chair. His limbs ached and sweat was pouring from his body. He staggered to the kitchen sink and poured himself glass after glass of ice-cold water. Never in his life had water tasted so good.

The air in the kitchen was oppressing him. He shuffled dizzily along the dark hall and out of the back door of the house. He found himself in a small field, thick with nettles and surrounded by a wall. There was a green wooden door set into the wall. He pushed it open and stepped into the churchyard. The air was scented and sweet. Roland leant against a tombstone and, as he did so, a chorus of chirping crickets rose up to greet him.

It seemed to Roland that they were rubbing their wings together, spelling out something in a weird Morse code.

Roland closed his eyes and covered them with his hands. The darkness was punctuated with stabbing flashes of red. When he opened them it was to see a large white cricket sitting on the tombstone. The cricket glared at him with pale green orbs. It rubbed its wings together drily and deliberately and started to rasp out his name in Morse.

* * *

That night, as he lay in the darkness of his bedroom, a breeze started up in the branches of the linden trees. A whispering, a rustling, which came nearer and nearer until it filled the room. He thought of angels' wings.

The shadow was in the corner, but this time he did not shrink away. He welcomed it. A bitter scent filled the room. Herbs? May blossom? What did it matter. She had suffered terribly, and now he must suffer too. The woman in the white dress moved towards him and he gazed into her beautiful eyes until he seemed to be drowning in them.

His pyjama jacket was open. The woman bent and gently – so gently – kissed him. Then she took a ring from her finger and laid it on his chest. She was laughing down at him when he closed his eyes.

He was drifting far away, back in time, the present becoming the past. Had he lived it, or was it a tale that had been told to him?

A young and beautiful girl from a farm on the hillside, betrothed to a young man who lived in the village. The ordering of material for a special dress, a dress to wear on her wedding day. And the tainted cloth for the dress, which came by horse and cart from London. The marriage hearse.

"And blights with plague the marriage hearse."

Which poem was that from?

And the young girl waiting to die, isolated with her family on a hillside farm. Her sweetheart dancing with a new love at the village wakes. So she put on the dress, the fateful wedding dress, and came down from the hillside one dark night to find him sleeping.

And that was how it started, he thought, as he tossed and turned, aching all over and running with sweat. That was how the plague came to the village.

He was drifting back now, back to when he was a small child, out playing in the street with the other children. The children had formed a circle round him and they were singing something . . .

Later, when Quinn came alone into the room, a dark shaddow still hovered in the corner. The pocket of posies, dangling on its cord, began to swing in the impetus of the draught from the door.

Quinn stared in horror at Roland, at the huge swelling under his armpit, and the swelling underneath his neck, which had knocked his head sideways. On Roland's chest, over his heart, was the livid ring of roses.

138

The red plague rash.

The leather pouch began to swing violently as a decaying stench filled the room. Quinn seized the pouch and ran downstairs with it. Sweating, he searched for matches and paraffin, and thrust the pouch deep into the fireplace. A tongue of flame leapt up, and then another licking and consuming the soft, writhing leather, and from somewhere, through centuries of time, a terrible scream was heard. Quinn crossed himself.

Their bright feast over, the flames dropped away from the charred and blackened pouch. Still kneeling, Quinn poked at it, and the ashes fell, powdery, into the hearth.

Quinn went upstairs, to find Roland sleeping peacefully. His face was no longer flushed, and the swellings on his neck and under his armpit has disappeared. There was no sign of the ring of roses on his chest, only Sydney, the cat, curled up into a ball and purring. For twenty-four hours he slept like a baby. When he awoke, it was to find Quinn sitting by his bedside. Quinn's hand was bandaged, and in a sling.

In the benign days of early autumn, Roland explored the churchyard. He was looking for a very old headstone, mentioned in the village guide. Eventually he found it, blank at the front from the weathering of hundreds of years and encrusted at the back with a mass of fossils, like round stone worms. New graves depressed him, but here the tombstones leaned tipsily in all directions. Old, weatherbeaten, grassed-over, they were, in some strange way, comforting.

And then he saw them, the two blackened headstones, near to the ivy-covered wall. The lettering had been worn away, but he could just make out the name on one stone,

"Rowland Swanna"

and on the other,

"Mary Teylor . . .

Lyk a shadow, so passes life"

And it was then that he realized the significance of the break in the lettering on the headstone in the cellar. That was all it had been – a discarded headstone, made use of at some later date by the village mason. Mary Teylor's body had been here all the time, next to the body of her sweetheart. Her kiss had sealed his fate and in death she had married him.

The headstones were blackened with age and sunken, and the tendrils which choked Mary Teylor's grave had long since encircled the grave of Rowland Swanna.

Poison ivy. Ring of roses. My love she laughs like the flowers.

In his heart, Roland felt a swell of pity for Mary Teylor. The finding of the pocket of posies had awakened inside the old stone cottage ancient feelings – feelings which should have been buried and dead. He had been lying in the same room that Rowland Swanna had lain in but that, he knew, was not the only reason she had haunted him.

And with the feeling of pity came a feeling of peace towards everyone – and a feeling of love for Quinn.

For though his jealousy of Quinn had echoed that of Mary Teylor, it was Quinn who had saved his life. Quinn who had burned his own hand when destroying the pocket of posies. Quinn who had banished the bitterness for ever. The next day was the first day of September, and Roland started at the new school.

ORDER FORM